Zathena
and the
Sky Pirates

Haley Newland

Zathena and the Sky Pirates

The text of this book is set in 12-point Arial

First Edition

The Account of 1545

In the days of the beginning of the nations, only the Rogoian capital stood steady. The great King and Queen Keiji ruled over all Rogoia. We Vermyrian lived with the Rogoians dwelling amongst their people. The King and Queen however, did not like our kind with our individuality. Our new name became "The Vermin." They believed us to be an unclean people. They took us from our homes and placed us in a land where the seasons changed erratically. The ones who stayed in their homeland, Rogoia, were slaughtered by the Rogoian officials. Their own kind! Our new land's seasons were so harsh that many of us grew sick and died within the first year. The ones who survived decided to embrace the name that was handed us, Vermin, and changed it to Vermyia, the name of our country. With this our main capital became, Vessaten, and we became known as Vermyians.

This is our brief history that all shall know,

Aleric Clement

Dear Citizens of Vermyria   1873

It is truly a tragedy that we have lost our greatest leaders as of late. King and Queen Miller of Vermyria have been declared deceased three months ago from today. They died from a poison that we cannot name, but that the guards of the castle, should have been able to detect. King Sebastian loved the Queen dearly and they will be solemnly missed. As of this time we are only aware of one such culprit who will remain nameless. We will capture this man so he will lay no harm on royalty again.

We are also proud to announce we are now able to assist the people of Vermyria in their affairs. This was all made possible by the late King and Queen themselves. Let us all be thankful for the help that they have provided for your beloved country.

Ragoian Official,

Nobel Guard Garreth

CHAPTER 1
It Begins

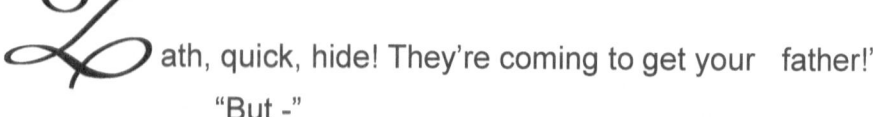ath, quick, hide! They're coming to get your father!"

"But -"

"Just do it!" I didn't know what was going on, but I did what my mother wanted. My mother had told me it was only a matter of time before my dad would disappear. I was so frightened then, I did not know what to do. Remington, my father was going to be taken away for a long time, and possibly even die.

I slid into my favorite hiding spot, a cabinet with a hole in the paneling for me to look out. I could hear pounding on the door as I sat huddled beside a burlap bag filled with something or other. I could only see my mother's feet as she paused in front of the cabinet, then proceeded to answer the door. I could hear men shouting, and my mother replying in fright. It's hard to remember the conversation from that day. I usually try not to think about it.

I heard the door bash against the threshold, and several pairs of boots rushed across our little house into our bedroom. A brief commotion ensued, with my father yelling in intense anger, and ended with a loud slam. Mother walked near the bedroom and let out a blood wrenching shriek as the men returned, dragging my father out, with his limp feet scuffing the floor. I had pressed my hands to my mouth and burst into tears, stifling a scream as I watched helplessly. My father's body disappeared from my view.

That was the last time I saw my father. I did not know who they were, or why they wanted him. My mother Luna and I thought the Raqoian officials wanted him for something more. After that, Luna would avoid speaking about Remington, for our lives only digressed from that day on.

Work was scarce in the city, so finding a good enough job to fit my mother's qualifications turned out being more difficult than I had thought possible. For a few weeks, my mother tried getting by, by picking pockets and stealing fruit in the marketplace. We learned to take care of each other on the big city streets. I would sneak into windows to unlock doors for her; playing the innocent card. I can still remember the musty smell of the dirty wet cobblestone as we ran down alleyways and hid scouting for our next mark.

I would see the other kids walking down the different roads with their fathers, or being carried by them. It made me feel completely out of place and alone. Secretly I wanted to be held, and told everything was going to be okay. I longed for my mother to do the same for me. I prayed so badly that she would hold me in her arms and whisper; *daddy is going to come home soon. He will read to you, and rock you to sleep, just like every night. He's only on a long vacation.*

I could always remember asking my mother that same dreadful question. "Mommy, where's daddy?" She would nervously glance around in distress, like she knew the answer but didn't quite know how to explain it.

"Away." She would always reply with that same beautiful charm in her voice. Her tone could calm any child, it was sugar coated, intriguing and hers. "He's in a better place now."

After a few weeks, however, she started disappearing. At first it was only for a couple of hours. Than for whole nights at a time, and I'd have to steal from the market by myself, which was much more difficult. Finally one night, she never came back. I spent the next decade just trying to survive alone.

One day, when I was about nine, I used my house as a base and I snuck out into the eastern sector marketplace. I had not eaten the day before, and I began to feel light headed. The market stalls were heavily guarded by Raqoian soldiers, with their polished armor and menacing helms, it looked nearly impossible to sneak fruit past them.

A short heavy-set man gawkily walked toward the spice vendor, his extravagant clothes trimmed with gold. I knew he had more than enough money to spare, he wouldn't mind missing a few simple money pouches. I followed my target from a distance, until he stopped near a small boy to buy the news. I used my opportunity and walked up behind him, trying to look nonchalant. Using a small blade, I cut the wire connecting the pouch to the oaf's belt.

As I slipped back into the crowd, I saw one of the guards looking at me in a suspicious manner. I didn't think he thought anything at the time, but I wasn't going to wait around. I made my way to the nearest alley and slipped in between buildings. I stopped suddenly hearing Mr. Moneybags furiously yelling about his lost purse. I looked behind me and saw the guard pointing towards where I last stood. Raqoian soldiers are always on every street of Versalen. They like to keep us citizens 'in check', which should really be the other way around.

The last time I could remember almost running into one after stealing, was when I was six. My mother was with me, and we ran straight home, locking the door behind us. We sat there in the dark, and when the soldier came we were silent, pretending no one was home as he knocked on our door.

"*I need to get home.*" The thought kept circulating through my mind, so I ran. I turned down different alley ways and through clothes on lines near houses. Soon I slowed down around Bederaux Street. I had a nervous, fluttering and eerie feeling haunting me.

I turned around thinking someone had followed me, but I was met with nothing, only shadow, and the gentle, shy breeze where maybe something like a specter had been closing in behind me. Whatever it was, it slipped away into the shadow of a nearby dilapidated building, silent as the cool breeze and the fluttering dead leaves floating across the road. The wind chilled my bones, as I felt shivers run through my nerves like lightning.

Walking up to my house I quickly ran in, locking the door behind me. My house was musty, dark and unkempt. The dingy curtains stayed drawn, for, if I ever raised them, the open room would have flooded with dust and dirt. Broken wooden chairs circulated the likewise scuffed table and on top, a single large Talea rose soaked in a dirty green vase.

This was my favorite flower; my father and I used to walk through the marketplace finding the right vendor that carried this rose. It was sort of like our game of scavenger hunt.

A loud knock could be heard from my front door, and my instincts at that time, told me to throw the money pouches in the nearby cupboard. I placed my hand on my dagger as I walked toward the door.

"Open the door lass," The Raqoian voice called back from behind the door; his voice muffled through his close helm. "We want to speak with you."

I stayed quiet, occasionally stopping my own breath. A louder knock was heard and my muscles jolted.

"We know you're in there." I would have asked them who they were but I knew the answer already. I stepped backward silently, and walked toward what used to be my parents' bedroom. Multiple knocks came, each one louder than the last. Locking my room's door reassured me of safety.

"Open the door!" I quickly hid under my parents' bed, too frightened to leave, but soon all was quiet. At the time, I thought they really had given up, and left. I crawled out from under the bed walking out of my room, leaving my dagger behind and then into the main room. I heard their muffled voices speaking lightly.

"These dumb peasants thinking they can take from us royal families." The walls began to shake when they kicked the door loose off its hinges. A group of soldiers invaded my home, metal boots crashed against the wooden floor, eager to attain the hidden cash.

One guard in metallic, onyx stone encrusted armor stopped in front of me, examining me. These men, who wear armor like this, represent the Noble guards. They are the ones that handle all the official royal affairs.

"Whose house is this?" His accent was strange. The other men started pulling shelves off of cupboards, scattering lingering dust. They wouldn't stop for anything, until they found what they came to look for.

"Uh," I stood paralyzed by fear, and felt unable to speak.

"This house belonged to former Mr. Kahara. Why are you occupying it?" I quickly backed away. Somberness withheld in his voice, "Or could you be his daughter?"

I tried to rejoinder. "His daughter...? Yes, I am." The man began pacing the scrutinized room, and occasionally he would analyze the ceiling. The worst thing about men in armor is, you can never see their true emotions, you can only quietly guess.

He spoke with empathy. "Where's your mother, child?" Without being able to run away, I felt claustrophobic. My heart shook from fear. I held the ends of my hair, messing with ringlets. "She's…" He looked back at me, giving his attention. "Dead. I think."

Another guard came up behind the Noble guard, placing his gauntlet on the paldron of the other. "Ehy, I know of this Mr. Kahara fellow. We didn't know of no daughter though." His metal close helm looked dead toward me. "We should've' killed her when we had the chance." At that very moment I thought I wouldn't live another day. I had a feeling that they were just going to kill me then, not care about a disposable law-breaking orphan girl. He pulled back his sword, ready to make a strike as the other soldiers walked up from behind me, facing toward the Noble guard.

The Noble guard discerningly reached behind him, pulling forward a poleaxe. He threw the other soldier behind himself, pinning him against the wall. Behind grinding teeth he said, "You do not kill without first being given orders."

"Et was only a mere joke!" He stifled.

The Noble guard tactfully stepped back, looking at the others. "Did you find the money?"

"Yes, sir." He took the money pouch from the guard, rattling it.

"Everything seems to be in order." He said as he viewed its containments. "Look lass. You can't live here anymore; the houses on this street are for the royal guards and soldiers. If your mother were here, I would have just let it go. It would have been our little secret; however, seeing you steal and living for free in this establishment, it can't continue any longer."

"Uh," I decided to agree to the circumstances, knowing that they normally do not spare lives like mine. I picked up some spear items and filled up a knapsack with them. I was still confused though, on one thing.

Half of the soldiers opened the door leaving, I followed behind as the Noble guard gestured me out. Stopping outside, I stopped to look at him. His helm gleamed in the sun. "You're not going to arrest me?" Half of the group had already walked away.

He laughed light heartedly, "Why would I arrest a little girl for trying to survive." He pulled out a gold coin piece from the pouch and tossed it carelessly to my palms. "Don't get caught again." I nodded my head as the other soldiers walked away. The Noble guard locked the door, bowed his head and followed the rest.

Evicted from the one place I peacefully lived with my parents. *How would my mother ever find me again?* That was the last thing I questioned that night.

Since then, I was too afraid to steal if a soldier was near. I became thinner and when I was about twelve I decided to just give up. Other children, with their parents, playing in the streets and buying toys, made me sick. I was glad to be an orphan at this point, because I knew the lies hiding behind the smiles of adults. They act loving but in my reality, they can never truly care.

*   *   *   *   *

The desert season of Suhan was nearly here. During this season, a ravenous heat devastated the land, killing crops. The swamp plants hibernated into the ground and then desserts form in Vermyria. Well I mean that is what locals talked about.

I met a woman in the marketplace that month, which changed my views on adults. This woman, who was lightly tanned, looked homely. Not the bad kind, the really lovely kind, with just a touch of wrinkles. She worked as a merchant in the eastern sector marketplace, under a striped tent.

Soldiers and guards didn't patrol in the morning, I realized. I was stopping by that day, to steal fruit, but then the lady saw me. Angry she asked, "Where's your parents?" Her accent was strange, like that of the Raqoian guard. I said nothing, just stood there blankly, astonished she noticed my presence. "I swear; your parents should be thrown in Verkatraz prison letting their raggedy child outside during the season of Sudan. You could faint from the heat!" At that time

I couldn't tell if she was being serious, rude, or speaking on my side. I would have said, *I am an orphan, and I'm not raggedy.* I hate using the word orphan however; I had to make my statement more personal.

"My parents are dead." After I was evicted, I started believing the worst had happened to my mother. I shed tears in front of her then, for that was first time I said it out loud, even to myself.

She seemed to have been glancing at my gaunt skeletal frame. She burst out, "Oh dear!" Tears in her eyes, she ran out from behind her market's stand. Squatting nearly to my height, she pushed my dirty hair away from my face, stroking it back. "I'm sorry darling, I didn't mean it."

She handed me fruit and said. "My friends call me Mae, but, if you'd like you can call me Gran-Gran. I live in a small one room house with my husband Bill. We need someone to watch our market stall at night, you could sleep here, if you'd like. I wish I could do so much more for you dear." Her smile tensed with nervousness. "I've always wanted children, but my body never let me."

This lady put her trust in me for no other good reason, then me being alone. After this conversation, she and I grew extremely close. In reality, it's like I adopted her. *I could never think about leaving Gran-Gran.*

She put me in Versalen primary schooling, so I would have someplace to go during the day, and I slept cozy in the marketplace at night. She gave me half of all the food she cooked, and I could eat fruit when I wanted. Really, after I turned thirteen, I started to love my life.

*   *   *   *   *

The desert season of Suhan had come and gone, now replaced with the Mudan season. During this, the Miller River overflows into the desert and tsunamis down poured the rest. Also, Kailu the river next to Versalen, our capital, and the place I call home, would deluge over the flood walls. This created swamp lands.

After the season change, Bill died at the age of seventy-two. I was fourteen and still at school when I heard the news. A group of kids were sitting at lunch when one of them slammed their hands on the table jumping upward. "Wanna know why I wasn't at school yesterday?"

"What? Why?" The boy next to him questioned.

"My dad came home and told me he had to drag an old man out of his house after dying from being sick. Then he told me I needed to stay home and help him clean the dead person."

The boy asked him in excitement."Who was this?"

"Bert... Bill..." He gazed around the room, "I don't really know." After hearing the news I ran out of school, telling the teachers I wanted to go play outside. I ran into the marketplace and Gran-Gran was sitting behind the market stand crying.

"Gran-Gran, what's wron-" I didn't have time to finish my sentence. She yelled furiously at me. "Get your things, and get out! I don't need you here! You are a nuisance!"

I felt heartbroken. The only adult that seemed to care was no longer there for me. This made me cry but I couldn't help my situation. I never went back to school after that. I couldn't dare face the students in my class, or the school's payments. I dropped out. I stayed thin after that and again, stealing food became my only option.

I would not have survived much longer because constant fog was making for cold days and freezing nights.

That was until I met Satomi. That day stands out more than any other in my memory.

"Hey...Are you okay?" I opened my eyes. Realizing I was lying on the cobblestone street, I placed my hands on the ground lifting myself up, while rubbing my eyes.

"What?" I asked curiously

"Um...Hi." it was a girl with extremely light blonde hair, silver like, pulled back into a ponytail, bangs falling over her eyebrows. Goggles lay on the top of her head. Her large almond eyes caught my attention. They were like a Raqoian's eyes. Her brown corset tightened her white, short sleeve blouse to her torso. Egg shell white and red Victorian bloomers for shorts, that cut off mid-thigh. Her boots were old and worn, tied halfway up her shin, the rest doubled over. She looked about sixteen years of age, so I thought at the time. "My name's Satomi. What's yours?"

"Zathena." I replied.

"It's nice to see someone who seems to be in the same situation as me. Are you all alone too?" She smiled at me then, but it quickly faded. "Er, I'm not trying to imply anything rude...I was just curious given the current circumstances." I nodded. It's not like every day I meet a girl my age. I would not have normally trusted someone I had just met, but there was a glow in her strange eyes that reminded me of my mother. It made me feel as if I had known Satomi my entire life.

"Uh? Oh yeah I'm alone thanks for asking."

"Well, I'm certain sitting out in this miserable weather doesn't sound like the most attractive of ideas. You should come with me. There's an orphanage I stay at that's owned by a couple of kind people. I think you'd like it there." She grabbed my hand and pulled me up. We ran straight to a place I did not even know existed, or at least was too blind to see. The reason why I had only stayed in one place was because most stories elders told me frightened me about the outside world. The Raqoian guards harassed anyone they wanted to and it was only getting worse.

*   *   *   *   *

While we ran through the streets I thought truly how grateful it was to meet this new stranger. We slowed down in front of a white Corinthian building. A sign out front painted black read "*Home for the Lost (orphanage)*". Satomi flung open the door

"Lewis!" The room was a very small place with two doors, one way in and out, the other was opened. Through the open door I could see a hallway with many different doors, but this one small room was lofty and almost palatial. I glimpsed around in awe.

"Lewis, this is Zathena." I focused at him. Lewis was a tall broad old man with white hair. He also had stubble on his chin and below his cheeks, and a scruffy white mustache. He was wearing a top hat and had on a gray wool tartan suit. Satomi continued with a sweet tone, "Can she stay with us? She has nowhere else to go."

"Oh! Of course, but first we have to know about her current living conditions." This man, Lewis, was asking me about my life? That upset me because it was hard for me to talk about this subject as it was. I stared at Satomi as her face lit up with a smile. I feel like she wanted to know as well. I started playing with my hair, twirling it. That is normally what I did every time someone asked me uncomfortable questions.

"Umm, well I do not really want to talk about it, all you really need to know is that I lived out in the streets since I was about fourteen." I looked away. It was too hard to look at someone and tell them what my past was like; especially if I did not know that person. Lewis saw that I was feeling uncomfortable about the question.

He turned to the other orphans in the room "Well I guess we can find out more in time after we earn her trust." Turning back to us Lewis stated, "So, where did Satomi find you, Zathena?"

She answered the question for me quickly. "I was walking out by the eastern sector marketplace, and she was sleeping on the corner in front of a dilapidated building."

Lewis commented, "You *by* yourself survived *much* longer than what some of these kids would have. Zathena, please remember; you are always welcome here whenever." He smiled genuinely.

I said quietly "Okay" Lewis walked to the opened hallway door. He gestured me to follow him.

"Well, come now, we have a room for you. If you ever get a job you can decorate it, or you can just work for me, but I'm cheap so don't think you will earn much." He said smirking.

I nodded "Thank you so much for letting me stay here."

Lewis smiled. "Oh don't mind it, it always happens."

I followed Lewis down the main hallway. We stopped in front of a narrow door. Lewis pushed the door open revealing a snug room with a bunk bed, hardwood floors and one red rug big enough to cover the bare floor, A large round oval window, a ledge lay in front of the window with a book shelf underneath it with dozens of books. "So do you like your new room?" I turned around, to see Satomi standing in the doorway.

I smiled nervously "Oh, yeah, of course. I am very happy I found a place to sleep." Satomi crossed her arms with a furious look on her face.

She rolled her eyes. "I'm not sure if you had noticed or not...But there's a big sign out front pointing right at the place. How could you miss it?"

I had a feeling she did not like me and I became nervous. "It's not that, I just don't like following rules, so I stayed away." The real truth is I never knew there was even a house for the orphans. I could not let her know that, though, considering I lived in this city for sixteen and a half years.

Satomi smirked. "Well, this is my room, too, so calm down. I should, however, have you know that those books over there are mine and I'd prefer if you didn't touch them. If I'm feeling generous someday, I might let you read some of my older ones." She must have felt like I was invading her space.

"Alright I understand." I laughed with uncertainty. I began to walk over to my bed, my long hair swayed as I walked, and brought out my bag I have been carrying with me. Well more like a journal and pencil. I turned my head to look at Satomi. She saw my journal held carelessly in my hands.

"Wait, is that your journal? If it is, I bet you've written many tales of your exploits. That...sounds rather interesting, actually." She faltered for a moment. "Sorry...I'm rambling."

I smiled "My life is a story Satomi and so is yours. It's just how you look at it." So just like that my story began.

I just hope it isn't the romantic type. Who would want to live one of those things? I like adventure and on this road, I think there will be plenty of it.

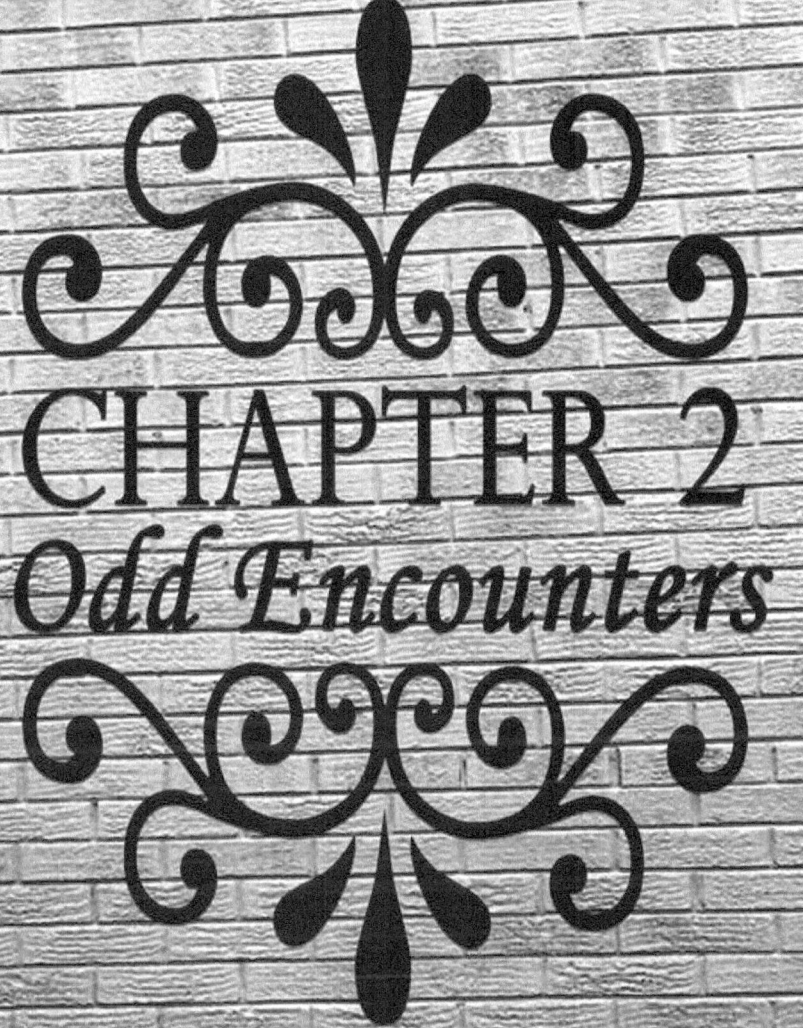

CHAPTER 2
Odd Encounters

I awoke the next morning as intense sunlight filled the room. The snug room became blurry as I rubbed my eyes. I sat up and leaned over the edge of my bunk. "Satomi," I called out "are you down there?"

"Yeah, I'm here." She called back.

Satomi was sitting on the side of her bed; she looked up at me smiling. "I think they're serving breakfast now," the girl remarked, while she glanced over at an almost rusted clock on a nearby desk. "Plus I'm sure the others will be happy to meet you."

I shrugged helplessly. "Alright," I climbed over the edge of the bunk bed and dropped down.

We both walked outside the room and passed a teen wearing a black top hat. He wore a red and white striped suit with a black tie under his black vest. I could feel his natural large blue-green eyes moving along with my every motion through the shade of his hat.

As we passed him Satomi leaned in whispering, "That's Zilpher Drax," Satomi looked back at him. He dropped his gaze from me and tilted his hat to cover his eyes. She looked back at me. "He's a bit shy. Don't take it personally."

I looked down at my feet and felt my cheeks blush a little. Not from liking him, mind you, but because he seemed so strange. *Who was this mysterious boy and why was he staring at me?* "Oh, that's strange." I replied uninterested.

We stopped at the end of the hallway and entered the door Zilpher had walked out. Through the door, was a comfortable, appointed high-raised living room. Half of the orphans stood around idle.

A small dainty looking lady with short brown hair, and white puffy shoulder long sleeved shirt tight at the wrist, and light purple corset that pulled in her torso, with a ruffled long skirt, and wearing a kind smile, strolled over to me. "Hello, Zathena, my husband had told me you arrived yesterday afternoon?"

I tilted my head. "Your *husband*?"

She nodded. "Lord Lewis is my husband."

I felt taken-back. "Oh, he did not mention you." I laughed slightly, "Or I would have known, I'm sorry."

She laughed a little. "My name's Tammy."

I heard the door creep open. Zilpher had walked in and was now standing in the corner of the room staring my way. I looked back at Tammy she was gesturing for me to walk closer to her. She declared in a loud voice, "Hello children and not-so-children! May I please have your attention?" Everyone stopped what they were doing and looked our way. "This is our new member of the orphanage, please make her feel welcome."

I said quietly, "Hi, I'm Zathena." Lewis walked over to his wife and me directly after.

He gestured toward a chubby boy in his teens. "This is Yomata." Yomata held darts in his hand, focusing on the board in front of him.

"Don't mind me, I'm playing darts." He said in a reply to Lewis. As he threw it, it curved and missed its target completely which caused him to sigh in exasperation.

"I'm kind of blind."

Zilpher leaned in from out of the darkness laughing. "What are you talking about?"

Yomata then threw the last two darts, getting a bull's eye each time. I stood looking astonished.

Tammy leaned in closer. "He's not really blind dear." She whispered. *Oooh,* I thought.

Zilpher leaned back into the darkness, and quietly recited.

> *"That my days have been a dream;*
> *Yet if hope has flown away*
> *In a night, or in a day,*
> *In a vision, or in none,*
> *Is it therefore the less gone?*
> *All that we see or seem*
> *Is but a dream within a dream."** (Poe, 1849)

I remembered when my father used to write poetry. This thought made me smile, picturing my family and I sitting around while listening to my father reciting poems all day, and creating some of his own. I stopped smiling after noticing Zilpher looking my way.

Lewis rolled his eyes in annoyance as he walked away. I followed right behind him stopping as he did. He smiled, gesturing towards the two dressed-a-like girls. "This is Jejuahn and Taeyeon. They are as close as sisters; they came to the orphanage the same day at age six." They were sitting on the floor, facing each other but their eyes toward me. They were probably annoyed at the fact that I had interrupted their conversation.

Jeju had deep red hair cut just below her shoulder. She had thin lips and almond shaped eyes. She wore a black and green long sari, and had on a jeweled headpiece that matched her friend, Taeyeon. Taeyeon had fare mid-dark skin with round eyes and dark brown short hair cut in layers. She wore a red and gold sari.

They both stood up and walked toward me. "Hi, Zathena." Jeju shook my hand while Taeyeon looked me up and down, staring at my old worn out desert style Bedouin clothing.

She smiled at me and said, "I'm glad you aren't on the streets any longer." She then embraced me with a hug.

"After breakfast we should hang out." Jeju suggested.

"Definitely!" Taeyeon added.

I nodded, "That would be fun." The girls strode out of the room after that, looking like royals as they exited into the dining room.

"Zathena, I need to go help my wife with the breakfast, please do make yourself at home." Lewis explained as he walked out of the room.

I looked to the far west of the room, behind the sofa next to a small easel stood a boy that looked more like he was a man. His hair was short and somewhat tired. He wore goggles over his eyes and seemed a bit creepy from far away. He was leaned against a white wall, holding a pad of paper while scanning the commotion. I walked up to him curious as to what he was doing.

"What are you-?"

His words cut me off, "My name is Jimmy, and I am capturing the moment." I glanced at his paper.

He already had drawn many different color strokes that faded into each other.

Although I had no clue as to what it would turn out to be, I complimented his work, "It looks nice, but how do you draw with it being so loud in here?"

He looked at me and laughed. "I haven't even started yet," He silenced my curiosity with, "shush". As soon as he said that the room became extremely quiet. I glanced around; I could see people talking but could not hear them.

I looked back over at Jimmy as he was staring down at his paper. I held a look of confusion on my face. He looked back at me smiled and said, "You just entered my brain for about ten seconds, congratulations." As he sat down to his easel to draw I started to back away slowly.

I turned around and saw a boy sitting in a wheelchair, with his hand inside of a strange black box with mysterious mechanical embellishments all over it, looking like he was trying very inefficiently to retrieve something. Suddenly the circular hole clasped around his hand, and he started struggling, flailing the box in the air. A few people looked over to him, and then looked away like it was no big deal.

I ran across the room to him. He looked very determined and serious. "You can you give me a hand, won't you?" he asked, annoyed.

"Okay? What do I do?" I said nervously.

He spoke and, nodded at two sides of the box. "Put your finger in the hemispheric reciprocation servo block and hold your thumb against the fulcrum release trigger" He yelled while still jerking his arm back and forth like it was going to be sliced off.

"What?" I yelled back.

"See that small group of pipes and buttons on the top here? Put your finger inside while holding your thumb on this switch here." He pointed to the inside of the box, while continuing to turn his hand from side to side inside the box and yanking.

"What are you talking about?" I questioned. "I'm not putting my finger in there! We'll both have our hands stuck in that stupid thing!"

"I think I'm starting to lose it!"

"Okay, okay!" I put my finger in the block of mechanisms and pressed on the trigger. The box started to click and whirr as the tight group of gears retreated from around the boy's hand.

"I got it!" he pulled out a tiny metal spike and sighed, "Almost lost it." He smiled happily at his award.

"Oh? I thought you meant you were going to lose your hand..."

"No, the Capspian Brain usually behaves erratically when you attempt to adjust the morality data spike. I had it under control, but it's always nice to have an extra hand."

"Okay... I still don't get it... You talk really complicated."

"It's simple, really, Raqoian tech. Uh... I'm Devin, by the way." He spoke confidently but sounded like a true weirdo.

"It's... nice to meet you." I smiled, still feeling annoyed.

"Kiasitu."

"What?"

"It's 'as to you' for short. The language of the people you call 'natives'. I'm something of an expert on the native city culture."

"Really? That's swell. Uh, well, I have to go..."

"Bye..." he said his smug and superior attitude had changed to an undertone of sadness; which made me feel like this sort of thing happened to him a lot.

I asked. "Sit with me at breakfast, okay?"

He suddenly perked up "Oh, yeah, sure."

Zilpher walked over to me, as he did I noticed how strange he looked. I had never seen someone quite, different as he. He stopped close to me. My gaze met his then I looked away.

He smiled, "I, had a feeling you would show up here." His accent was different from anyone I had met as well. Not quite of the Vermyrian decent, yet not Raqoian. I looked at him once more.

"What?" I said confused.

"If you have free time today, would you like to go on a walk with me?" I smiled but the truth was I really did not want to go anywhere with him he seemed too mysterious to be near alone.

I moved my fingers through my bangs placing my hair behind my ear. "I'll have to think about it."

*Poe, E. A. (1849). *Dream within a dream.*

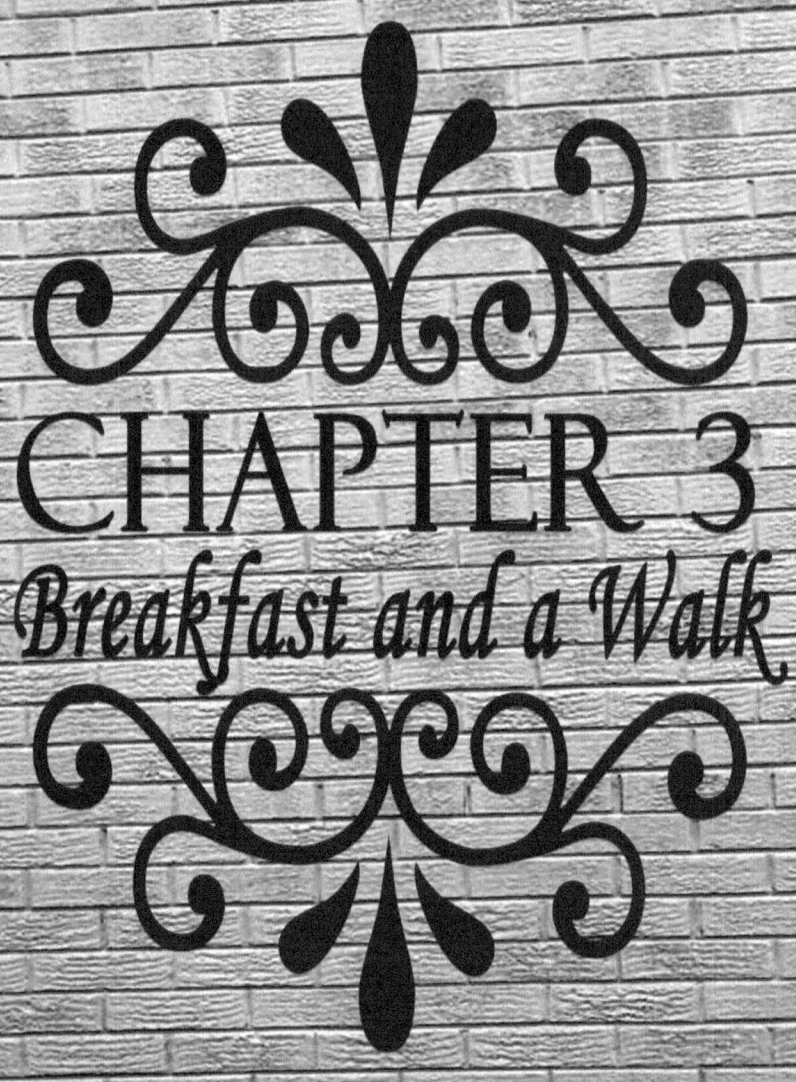

CHAPTER 3
Breakfast and a Walk

*A*t that moment I heard a loud ringing and jumped. I looked behind me at the opened dining room door.

Zilpher spoke next to me, laughing, "They ring the bell when breakfast is served."

He walked me into the dining room. Inside the rectangular room were three long tables, enough to fit eight chairs. The walls were decked in an understated candy stripe with a white border over a simple red bottom half, and warmly lit by elegant gold wall lights shaped like flowers, spaced enough for a minimal and cozy glow.

Tammy stood next to Lewis; his tall figure next to her small petite body; made them look like they were made for each other. Jeju sat next to Taeyeon and had called me over. "Zathena! We saved you a seat."

I nodded my head, turning to look at Zilpher. "I'll try to talk with you later." I walked over to the middle table and sat down next to the two girls. Devin wheeled up behind me mumbling something as he pulled up to the table.

Zilpher sat in front of me next to Jimmy who was still drawing in his book. I looked around to see if I noticed any new faces. That's when I found a new group of people who sat at the other two tables. They looked at each other smirking.

"Oh," I declared, "who are those people?"

"You really don't need to know." Taeyeon replied.

"Why?"

Jimmy looked up. "We don't talk..."

Jeju added. "You don't need to know the likes of them."

Devin laughed quirkily. "They eat walruses." I stared at him in disbelief.

Zilpher laughed, "What? No." he added, still laughing. "They all believe they're superior to us because of signing papers to become part of the Raqoian guard."

Tammy held plates of food while walking to our table. She placed multiple servings in front of each person. Naan, orange chicken placed on top of white rice and what looked like sparkling cranberry juice, next to that, water. It had been a long time since I had ever eaten something this nice and I thought I would never again.

Lewis walked over to his wife, and as she placed a dish in front of me he asked, "We're having our weekly game of Takraw this evening. Would you like to join us, Zathena?" Devin perked up, nodding that I should go.

"I guess so..." I said; it had been a while since anyone asked me to play a sports game with them, and I was actually very excited.

When the room was silent and people had ended their prayers, everyone started eating. I really didn't feel like eating and for some reason, I just couldn't bring myself to. I started to pick at my food while my head rested on my hand. Satomi looked over at me from beside Jeju. "Zathena?" I glanced over. "Why aren't you eating? It tastes good I promise. I usually help prepare it."

I started laughing. "It isn't that, Satomi." I tried the rice and the naan. *Just to make Satomi feel better,* I thought.

After we ate, we took our plates to the front.

"Hey, Zathena?" Satomi walked up beside me and tapped my shoulder in an effort to grab my attention. "Do you enjoy it here?"

"Yea, why wouldn't I" I nodded.

"Well...I was just wondering if you had anything planned for today." Satomi smiled.

"I think Taeyeon and Jeju wanted to hang out with me."

Satomi flashed an awkward and apologetic smile. "Oh, I see...Sorry." she apologized. "I'll see you this afternoon?"

"Of course!" I exaggerated. She flashed an awkward smile before leaving. I knew she was upset, but I didn't leave after her. I hope she wasn't too upset.

My ragged dress felt rough as I held it in my hand. *Of course...* I thought. *Why did I say it like that? I don't even know where their room is.* Devin wheeled up next to me.

"Do you know where their room is?" I asked suddenly, probably too quickly. I felt like he thought I was implying rudeness.

"Yeah, it's the second door of the west wing. You might want to take this with you." he handed me a stickman. "It's a ward against cooties. You don't seem like the frilly type"

"What? I don't want this." I said annoyed pushing it away from me.

"No…" He stammered. "You must! They'll even paint my toe nails if they can get a hold of me. Wanna see?" he acted like he was about to pull up his pant leg

"Uh, absolutely not, thanks." I suddenly changed the topic. "They have a crafting room here?"

"Yeah, I know it's for kids but I like to tinker and mess around. Would you like to-"

"Uh," I stuttered. "No, that's okay; I've never done anything like that before... Anyway, I've got to go upstairs. I'll talk to you later"

As I walked to their room, I couldn't stop thinking about how awkward Devin had sounded. He was a bit nice but so incredibly strange.

I knocked on Taeyeon's and Jeju's door. "Come in." I heard Taeyeon yell. I opened the door slowly revealing an en suite painted blue and a light green. A small round table sat in the middle of the floor in front of two different decorated beds, both to fit their own style. An oil lamp hung from the ceiling. They sat on pillows that lay beside the table.

Jeju had been painting Taeyeon's fingernails. "Come sit by us," Taeyeon said, while she motioned next to her.

Jeju asked excitedly. "Can we give you a makeover?"

I laughed with uncertainty. "I have never worn makeup before. I don't really know how it would turn out." I looked down at my Bedouin clothes and realized Taeyeon's facial expression had been a bit right. How did I go all of this time without realizing just how grimy my clothes had looked and felt?

Taeyeon smiled. "That's okay. Do you mind if we give you one of our old Sari's? I think you would look better in my old black and gold one."

Jeju nodded. "It would be perfect. Wait here." She stood up and walked to her closet pulling out a black and gold sari.

Taeyeon was blowing on her fingernails in an effort to dry them. She asked, "Could I practice my hair styling techniques on you? I have done it before and I think you would look just darling with layers!"

"That sounds interesting… alright."

Jeju glared at my long hair. "You are getting this complete makeover whether you like it or not!"

Taeyeon began brushing my hair, and cutting it in the finest of layers.

My hair was now down three inches past my shoulder. Jeju handed me a mirror. When I saw myself I quickly sat the mirror back down. I slowly lifted it and looked back startled. The hair that used to be tangled, long and in a hot mess was now luxurious. I stared at myself for a moment in disbelief. I quietly muttered, "I look just like my mother."

"Not done yet." Taeyeon hissed. Jeju handed me the sari and pointed to the half-bath. "Go get dressed." she said smiling.

I stepped into my long skirt, pulling the belly shirt over my head, draping the sari loose around my slim body. In the mirror I had seen the gold and black tint of the dress and how it casually laid on one of my shoulders.

I walked outside of the bathroom modeling. Jeju stood staring at me, tilting her head from side to side thinking. She then reached gently into her closet in curiosity, fumbling pushing clothes over. She pulled out a dark brown corset, with a lack of remembrance. "Put this on over it, I think this will make the look your own." I wrapped the corset around my skinny torso, tightening it.

"You are really pretty!" Taeyeon exclaimed. She then started to pull out block mascara from her bag, holding it up. "It can't be a proper makeover without makeup." She laughed. Taeyeon stood up, walking over and showed me how to apply it. "Look, I hope you wear this every day. Think of it like, your face is the canvas and you are the artist. Just brush your eyelashes with it."

She finished the last brush stroke, putting the brush back inside the case. Then placed it back in the small leather pouch she first had out. Jeju put the mirror back in front of me. "The mascara makes your eyes look amazing!"

I stared at myself in the mirror for a while, not understanding how closely I resembled my mother. I grabbed the mirror and looked closer at myself. I smiled from the thought; but then after seeing my mother smiling back at me, I put it down. Jeju gave me the block mascara smiling, "Keep this, every woman should wear makeup."

"Thank you so much, really you have no idea how grateful I am for these gifts."

Taeyeon smiled, "After living on the streets for as long as you did; you deserve them." I left the room shortly after that, with a smile on my face, the second moment in a short while that I could remember.

I walked back down the hallway. Passing girls dressed in white with black buttons, all glaring at me as if I had done something wrong. I felt someone grab my arm. "Zathena." I turned around not knowing who had spoken. Zilpher looked shocked. "You look gorgeous." I looked down, trying to conceal my smile. "Thanks."

"Would you like to go on a walk with me? I'd like to get to know you."

"That would be fun." I said excitingly. I followed him down the hallway and out the big doors.

The crisp air felt cool against my warm face, with the scent of spring. The town was buzzing with conversations from hundreds of people, all walking in different ways. Every way I looked, I spotted different people speaking all sorts of languages. Most of them; it was hard to decipher where they had come from; let alone what language they spoke. Their clothes were the only thing that helped me tell them apart from other nationalities. The city seemed large with tall buildings. The cobblestone street beneath me was new and seemed to have been polished.

We walked beside each other headed north to the market place. Zilpher glanced over at me. "When I was younger, my mother used to walk with me down this vary same road every morning, to get food for our household."

I looked up at him. He was looking straight ahead. "What ever happened to her?"

"I have no clue. I ran away after my father died."

I looked straight ahead. "I'm sorry, I know how that feels. My father died before my mother left."

"What was she like, your mother?"

I laughed, feeling nervous. Telling people about my parents always leaves me feeling uncomfortable. "She was nice, kind and loving. The type a mother should be, sure she didn't have ten years of schooling but who really needs that. She loved my father and me so much, that she did whatever it took to feed me after he was gone."

"Really, how did you survive on your own?"

"I lived in the marketplace with a vender." My voice trailed off. A hard look of disappointment was visible on my face.

"Is that why you never came to live in the orphanage?"

"Yea, I... I couldn't live there. I loved her; she was the nicest adult I ever had the opportunity to meet."

"I'm sorry, is she still alive?" Zilpher asked, sincerely.

"Yea, she is. I was always in her way. I left her, and quit my schooling at age thirteen."

"She's alive then. Does she still work in the market place?" I nodded. "Well then," Zilpher stated, courageously. "I must meet this dear woman who helped a young lady survive the city streets."

"I don't know if that's such a goo-" Before I could finish my sentence, Zilpher grabbed me by the hand and pulled me away.

We ran to the end of the market place stopping in front of a food tent. A little old lady sat behind a food table. I don't know what made him stop here, I never told him what she looked like, but I'm guessing he understood the situation seeing that she was the only older lady there. It was like, he knew this was Mae. I felt embarrassed to stand in front of her, but I'm glad I faced my belittling fears.

"Hello, Mrs. Twiddley." She was a small dumpy lady with short white hair and hazel eyes. Her wrinkles and fine thin lips told her age well. Zilpher seemed to hold back a laugh smiling from amusement.

"Where have you been? I was wondering about you." She stood with her arms crossed.

"I'm sorry Gran-Gran I didn't think you would care, I-"

"You could have at least told me if you were living a fine life!" She cut my words off with what sounded like a screeching laughter.

"I'm sorry; I now live in the orphanage."

She let out a thunderous, yet mild-toned laugh and said, "Well I say good riddance to you! No but really, I'm glad you have a place to sleep." She nodded.

"Oh Gran-Gran, I've missed you." I laughed.

"So out with it, did you come here for food or to chat?"

Zilpher spoke up, after what seemed like hours of letting me do the talking. "I'm glad you kept this young lady well fed, it's hard to live life on these streets without a bit of help."

"Don't think me child; it was because of my husband's understanding. I wouldn't have been able to provide for her on my own." Her eyes turned watery with a shimmer, and her eyelids looked red compared to her pale skin. Zilpher saw this too, and looked slightly startled to setting her off suddenly.

I changed the subject, helping her to not cry. "Uh, well what new food have you got?"

"Well, maybe I just like your company! Here is what was harvested by my goons." She picked up a basket from behind her chair and sat it on the table. "Oh what happened there?" She said, touching the basket. "Oh; I thought it was broken."

I looked inside the basket. "Uh, Gran-Gran there's a package of Walrus meat in here."

"Really,? Oh speaking of walruses. Look over there at that man." I looked behind me noticing a heavy set man with a white bushy mustache covering his mouth, "He looks like a walrus!" She declared laughing. I could not help but to join in, "Gran-Gran! That's mean! Here take this money." I said while handing her very small change. "I'll take this peach."

Mrs. Twiddley handed me the peach and said. "You better not leave here without a hug." I handed Zilpher the peach and walked behind the table to embrace her. Her small body felt comforting to hold.

I kissed her on the cheek. "I love you Gran-Gran."

"Please stay safe." She replied as I walked away.

Zilpher nudged me. "Is she really your Grandma?"

I laughed, "No, I adopted her."

He replied jokingly, "Oh because that makes sense." He tossed me a golden peach.

"Well, yea. So what was your mother like?"

"The same as yours really, I know I broke her heart when I left, but I needed to leave."

I stopped near a small table and sat in one of the chairs. "What was the true reason you left?"

Zilpher sat across from me. "My baby sister was crying because my father was being taken away. I ran outside of the house to stop them, but as soon as I did... after they noticed me, the guards murdered him in the alleyway. I felt like the only reason he was murdered was because of me and what I did. It was my entire fault. If I had just... walked away or never chased after him, they wouldn't have killed him. I knew I would have never been able to tell my baby sister what I had seen, so I ran." Zilpher sounded almost to the brink of tears.

I felt a lump forming in my throat. I stared down at my lap. "None of that was your fault. The guards have more power than they should."

Zilpher looked away, "I know."

Just then I remembered something strange, "That same morning, on my father's death," I looked up only to see Zilpher staring back at me. "It's hard to remember, but I know I had a friend over, and he too ran outside of the house looking for my father."

Zilpher laid his hand on mine. His touch surprised me. "There is something I need to tell-," His voice cut off as the streets became louder. On a different ground level below me an old dark skinned man with a white beard stood in the middle of the plaza. A metallic black armored Raqoian Noble ran up to the old man grabbing him by his shirt collar, shouting at him in a language I have never heard.

Zilpher's sad expression turned to calm rage, as if he could understand the fight commencing below us. "Please wait here." He said firmly. He ran straight down to the guard, shouting in Raqoian.

I sat there wondering what he could have been trying to tell me. I began to feel light headed. I kept my eye on Zilpher scared the Noble might fight him.

I heard a metal chair slide as someone sat in it. I looked in curiosity. It was a man his black messy hair short and somewhat spiked. Small almond eyes stared forward at the argument down below. A slight grin protruded the corner of his lips. He wore dark brown pants, his shirt white with a vintage gold vest over top and a leather spaulder covering his right arm.

As he peered over at me, I looked away sinking slightly in my chair in a hope to disappear. I felt more than uncomfortable when this person I have never met, nor seen before sat next to me. I continued my gaze toward Zilpher. The guard started yelling at him. I tried to pay closer attention wishing I could understand the words they were saying.

I looked to the wall on my right; arrest warrants hung advertising convicts from around the country.

"So… have you ever been forced to steal from people or is it something you willingly do?" I glanced over at the stranger; he was leaning with his elbows on his knees. Had he noticed that I stole something?

Stuttering, I asked "Uhh, excuse me?" He looked away from me and stared forward.

"You stole from my brother once. Took all he could afford." He stared at me once more, intently. He had a scar on the right side of his face stretching from his ear to his chin. His eyes were a light blue, and shimmering nonetheless.

That's when I noticed who he was. My mother used to read about him from the airship pirate book she owned. "The dashingly sky pirate Aruno." She would call him.

I became tense, my eyes widened; shocked and alarmed from my discovery. I scraped up the courage to say, "I think you may have me confused." His expression turned to rage. I flinched as he stood up. The chair fell behind him as he calmly walked away and disappeared down a side alley.

CHAPTER 4

A Visitor

Zilpher walked back up the path and sat down next to me. He seemed concerned.

I asked shyly. "What happened?" I was a bit out of it. My thoughts kept circling back to Aruno.

"The Raqoian guards have been acting out more since the king's arrival. This vary same thing happened yesterday as well, I'm sick of it." He looked over at me, and I could see the anger in his expression. "He was assaulted because of his former nationality." He heavily sighed in exasperation. I cut his thoughts off entirely when I changed the subject.

"Once you left, this weird man came and sat down next to me. He was angry when I didn't answer his questions."

He looked astonished. "What? Who? What did he look like?" I explained the situation in short detail, Zilpher seemed confused and walked over near the arrest warrants which hung on the wall. He ripped a page off of the wall, "Aruno..." Zilpher walked back, placing it on the table in front of me, "Did you steal from his brother?"

I became defensive. "No! Well... I don't exactly know." I picked up the paper, examining it. "But if I had," I thought about it for a moment then put the warrant back down. "I couldn't tell him that! I didn't know what he could have done."

"Hmm... I understand." He sat back down across from me. "You're fine," He smiled. "Just promise me you won't steal anymore. You have friends now that care about you and they don't want to see you get hurt."

I slowly nodded, "I guess you're right." This really made me curious about what he was going to tell me before. We sat there for a moment when a small girl with large blue wide set eyes and blonde hair ran from behind me, toward Zilpher

"Zilpher!" She jumped up wanting to hug him. After he hugged her she swayed on her heel, her light purple dress flowed. "Did cha hear? Did cha hear?"

"No I didn't; what is it Evian?" Zilpher replied laughing. Evian circled around and sat next to me in what used to be Aruno's seat.

"Orfeo is giving a speech today at four o'clock to anyone willing to listen."

"Oh really? That sounds truly wonderful. Are you going?"

With puppy dog eyes she looked at Zilpher and with a sweet tone she replied. "Mama told me I can't go unless someone goes with me."

"Oh did she?"

"Would you..." She glanced down and back up again. "Go with me?"

"Alright, Evian" Zilpher looked over at me. "Would you like to go with us?"

"That sounds alright." I had only ever seen Orfeo in propaganda and satirical paintings around the town, but never in person. This was an opportunity to really meet the new ruler, and listen to what he has to say.

"Come on, Come on." She grabbed Zilpher by the sleeve and led him to the castle's stadium. "The coliseum is too small! If we don't make it on time, they might close the doors!"

We stood in front of the large coliseum gates. Two tall sturdy armored men stood beside the big metal doors gesturing people inside. "Oy! Keep it goin'." a man yelled muffled behind his armor helmet. I couldn't tell which one it was, they were all gesturing the same way, as if they had rehearsed. And soon it did not matter.

Inside the gate stood thousands of people, all trying to get to the front of the crowd. The coliseum was enclosed by other's houses stretching around the back. People huddled around the large platform in front of the castle.

As the line slowed I looked around in caution. I could tell that many more people than me disapproved of Orfeo ruling over our country. People were shouting ridicule at the very place the new ruler would stand. There were armored guards posted on either side of the stage, and on the stairs behind leading to the castle. The Imperial flags of Raqoia- black crows embodied in red-hung from all sides and corners of the stadium. Large concrete benches lined the sides parallel from each other. Others, mostly the old, brought their own chairs to sit closer.

Zilpher looked at me with a kind smile, despite the former conflict he witnessed. I fell in step with Zilpher as the line started moving again. I would have never been able to stand up for another person the way he did. I looked up to him for this. This was something that I hated about myself. Not being emotionally strong to stand up for others especially the ones I love.

"This is going to be interesting." He grinned.

We stopped in front of an empty section in the benches. Evian sat down first, followed by Zilpher and myself. We had a good side view of the stage.

Zilpher studied the crowd. "These people don't really seem to like the king." He turned his head towards me. "It's a shame, isn't it?" He said with a sly smile.

"It's a shame that they hate their new ruler?" I asked confused.

"I think they should hear what he has to say, before they go make judgments."

"You mean like the rumor of how he killed his parents?"

"Who told you that?" He started laughing.

"A lot of people talk about it in the market place."

"Who really knows?" He turned and looked at Evian who was smiling from ear to ear. Looking at the swarming crowd below, and obviously unaware of our discussion.

The crowd shouted in an uproar of voices. Some yelling, "Get back to your own country!" Others yelled, "We want to see you die!" Their taunts made me let out a nervous laugh, because I wish I had the guts to tell him off as well. Zilpher looked confused.

More uproar, the crowd growing louder and louder, more shouts and condescension arose. Zilpher looked concerned for Evian hearing the foul language.

The new King walked slowly up to the main platform, his arms behind his back and his nose in the air. Orfeo stood tall and strong built. He had a long round shaped face with deep-set eyes. His low inner half arched brows along with pointed nose and thin lips gave him almost a sinister look. He had coal black hair to his shoulders. He wore the Raqoian empire seal along with others on his black and crimson red military uniform.

He looked slowly from one side of the crowd to the other. He paused, his gaze directly at me. I could not look him straight in the eyes and I had a feeling that he was staring right through me. He looked away, staring at the crowd now. His voice was loud and authoritative.

"My good Vermyrians" The unruly crowd suddenly cut him off with a cacophony of anger. The guards lining the walls and circling around Orfeo took it upon themselves to threaten the crowd with their weapons. Orfeo signaled to the guards to stand down he didn't want an escalation of violence.

"Eleven months have passed since the merger of the Nobles of our fine countries of Vermyria and Raqoia." As he finished the sentence the crowd began to again heckle, boo and express anger at this perceived false arrangement of their world. This was a problem especially because Vermyria had no true Noble house aside from the royals. The new joint house created was either Raqoian or Raqoian sympathizers from Vermyria, no real representation for the people of Vermyria.

Orfeo wanting to quell these concerns continued with "I understand the fear and distrust of the merger of our countries. I understand that some of you would see the new peacekeepers as occupiers, but I assure you they are no more than what their name implies. They are only here to make sure the public stays safe in this time of change and reduce conflict by their presents."

"I want you to know that as you accept my kingship, I shall also accept you. I for you good people am no longer a royal Raqoian, for I am one of you. I will endeavor for you not to be disadvantaged by a partnership with our bigger cousin, Raqoia, but for you to be aided by this partnership. I hope to see you as the new example of what our empire can rightfully be."

"Raqoia wishes to show support of Vermyria and end our long fought rivalries. We will fully accept your royals into our systems of governing along with the Vermyrians we have accepted" The response this time wasn't anger like before, some of the crowd reacted positively.

"I know that our Raqoian guards and soldiers in the role of peace keepers shall hold themselves to a standard befitting their name. I have heard of stories of discrimination against the Vermyrian people, these are blatantly false rumors spread by ones who do not have your good interests in mind. Our peacekeepers are held to the highest standers and reports of wrong doing are unsubstantiated.

"If at some point there is proof that a discriminatory action has taken place the punishment for that Raqoian offender will be quick justly and severely dealt with."

The crowd reacted with murmurs amongst themselves. How dare a person say all these lies! Had a guard that day not only yell at some bloke only for the color of his skin, but also threaten him? This was so aggravating!

I stared at Zilpher, who continued to have a look of concern. I had so many feelings boiling inside I couldn't even comprehend. He was speaking with so much sincerity I thought maybe the guard from earlier had been reprimanded. But throughout my life, I was taught that Raqoian people were racist, and abusive without repercussion.

I also knew this is what he wanted. He knew that people had witnessed accounts like this also, but his words made all the people believe there was nothing wrong with it, that it was all in the past.

I felt a powerful anxiety well up in me; I don't want his seeming lies to be propagated. I needed to get out of there; I couldn't bear hear any more of this. I stood up slowly, Zilpher grabbed my hand. "Zathena what are you doing? You can't just leave." I scanned the crowd.

"Watch me." I replied; my words left lingering in silence. I walked down the stairs from my seat. Zilpher followed behind me, holding little Evian by her hand. I walked the path I took to get there, steering clear of standing people. Some were fanning themselves from the heat.

The exits were flanked by guards in light, segmented plate armor, steam powered gauntlets which augmented their strength, and helmets covered their faces except with an opening for their mouth. They carried steam poleaxes; deadly crowd control weapons that jettisoned hot steam prepared in connected packs at their back.

I stopped as one guard blocked me at the entrance, looming menacingly at me, and his gauntlets vented steam as he tightened his grip around the poleaxe.

"Nobody leaves during the King's speech" he snarled "get back to your seat, peasant."

I had not noticed before that Orfeo had stopped talking, or the fact that everyone turned their backs to look at me. "You there! Why on such a glorious day like this, would you ever want to leave? If you have some objection, out with it."

My heart pounded in my chest. Surely he was not talking to me. I turned around; my eyes still could not meet his gaze. Everyone had their backs to Orfeo staring in my direction. I felt a lump forming in the back of my throat.

"You are a liar, Orfeo!"

"Whatever for?" He held a devilish grin. He was thinking up new ways to counteract my words and to ridicule me for them. So I prepared myself to say more than needed.

"Today one of your men attacked an elder man *for* the color of his skin. How can you stand up there talking about equality when you, *yourself* let it happen. You're feeding these people your carefully crafted falsehoods!" I looked around the crowd. "People, don't believe this deadbeat bunko artist!"

The entire coliseum gasped in horror as my final words were said, all thought I would be killed on the spot. Zilpher stood slightly in front of me, glaring at Orfeo and the entirety of the crowd. He grabbed my trembling hand, sensing my fear, as well as I of his own. I could not believe what had just slipped out of my mouth. I must have been the craziest person in that stadium, but I liked the feeling. Orfeo drew his head back laughing, "I assure you that I would not have let it happen. If I stood nearby and seen this atrocious behavior being displayed, I would have had that guard arrested!" His voice changed from cheerful to angry within an instant. "But you did not see this man's face, did you? How did you know he was not Vermyrian, working for our government?" His questions were rhetorical. Everyone in the stadium knew that Raqoian guards do not show their faces, even in the hottest of Suhan days.

Zilpher whispered in my ear. "Let's get out of here."

I let go of his hand and turned around, gates still closed.

"Let them through." Orfeo declared, thinking he had won. The crowd erupted into cheerful applause.

Some started yelling, "Fighting!" others yelled, "Tell him like it is!" Orfeo looked shocked. Then a chant broke out among the crowd, "Deadbeat! Deadbeat! Deadbeat!" Zilpher grabbed my hand, as the three of us ran off together.

"You've really upset the king; I think we need to get back to the orphanage."

"What I said back there... I honestly did not think people would agree with me, or really care about what I had to say." I really didn't! I could not believe those words slipped my mouth.

"Don't be so hard on yourself; everyone felt the same way as you. The Raqoian people have always expressed hatred towards other nationalities."

Evian looked up at Zilpher "Zilpher... I'm scared. Why would she be so mean to him?"

"It's alright Evian. Nothing will happen to you." Zilpher turned to look at me. "First we need to get her home."

We stopped in front of a short concrete apartment complex. The door was a little bit higher than the last stair, and Zilpher had previous knowledge of which when he opened the front door, letting himself in. This was not proper, was he somehow related to this child? As I waited for Zilpher, I kept looking behind me, nearly jumping at everyone passing. Had the speech ended early, with people returning to their homes? The entire situation kept my head spinning. Thankfully however Zilpher returned soon, strolling out of the house and closing the door behind him.

"Are you and Evian related; is that how you know her?" I wasn't trying to make accusations but Zilpher briefly flashed a shrewd look.

"No, I'm close to her parents. When I was younger, I was put in secondary schooling. They let me stay with them."

"Oh-" Again he spoke, this time with anxiety in his voice.

"Zathena, I need to tell you about," He paused, nervously looking forward. "That day, I mean..." He turned his head towards me. "I'm your brother."

"My...brother?" I paused to think " I don't... remember..." I didn't remember having a brother, the child that ran away from my home, I always thought was one of my friends.

I would have lost him when I was young, and I had pushed everything out of my memory from those hazy days. He quickly stated "I won't blame you for not remembering me, we were separated at a young age when the guards came and took our father." He smiled at me, "But I could never forget you."

I thought for a few seconds then made up my mind, "Yea, I vaguely remember an older boy that day, when my father was taken" I said fine and unsure. Then I thought; how could he be lying? He knows those final moments of my childhood well. *He even knows how the rest of the family was separated.* This was enough proof for me to believe him.

Back at the orphanage, after what felt like hours, I passed the lobby entrance and entered into the east corridor. A boy ran into me, full force as I turned the corner. As I fell down, he ran off yelling, "Watch where you walkin' brat!" I stood up dizzily and brushed my hands on my dress. What an imbecile. If he had just moved over some he wouldn't have ran into me. I straightened my hair, walking once more to my room. I creaked my door open just enough to walk through.

This day had gone better than expected. I still felt nervous and anxious from my outbursts. If I had started a riot, I might have put them all in danger. *Oh, I really hope I didn't.* I had my arms crossed and stared out of the window. The sun was beginning to set over the horizon. *How long was I gone today? My days used to be so drawn out, now that I have things to do, it seems my days are growing shorter.* I wondered if that's how the rest of the world viewed it.

Satomi came strolling in the room, confusion fell on her face. Her hair was brown and pulled back in a ponytail, bangs stopped just under her eyebrow. She wore silver painted goggles on the top of her head; a short white sleeve shirt and brown shorts over her candy stripe leggings she had worn before. "Zathena you missed the ball game!"

Oh no I completely forgot! "I am so sorry! Satomi I forgot!"

Satomi gave a caring smile. "It's alright, not a lot of people showed up because of Orfeo's speech anyway." Satomi plopped down onto her bed, once she caught my attention she burst into surprise. "Did you hear about the lunatic that started a riot?"

I shouted, "What!" Horror changed my expression.

"Yeah! Orfeo had to bring in the soldiers. Lewis told me they still haven't found the couple that committed the crime."

"Wow, that's insane." My facial expression stayed calm, but my nerves tensed.

"Well, Lewis told me to do chores today, but after, I'm going to the market. Maybe you can come with me?"

"I don't know about that... I was gone all day. I think I need to rest."

"Do you have anything in mind for me to get while I'm out?"

"Oh no, I'm fine." I replied anxiously.

"Alright, suit yourself!" She said with a little laughter.

Satomi left just as fast as she arrived. My only thoughts that followed were about the speech. *How could I be so stupid? I put myself and others in danger.* These thoughts soon followed with, *Soldiers? He had to bring in soldiers? The riot must have really been violent.* I glanced around the room. *I need to get my mind off of this stupid nonsense,* I thought.

I walked over to my bed pulling out a book that lay underneath it. I sat near the open window, the air cold as it touched my face. The book was titled, *Airship Pirates.* The page I left off on, marked by a single old picture I had kept for years. It was frail and creased. The picture was of the family and me sitting around an old draught table; my mother, father, and I. A smile creased across my mouth when I looked at my mother. I remember how her smile would always light up a room.

I squinted at the creases, my brother, Zilpher, was not in the photo. He claimed to be my brother, then why was he not sitting next to us. Confusion crushed me for a moment.

I looked at the page I left off on. It was a photo of the Ofeliya; a large, famous dirigible that was proved missing decades ago. I flipped through the pages, Aruno's airship; the Annabeth was drawn vividly stretching across two pages.

A loud explosion slightly shook my room. *What was that?* I glanced outside, the streets grew darker, and their lights turned on, illuminating mysteriously. Trees lined the streets and some sidewalks. Towers loomed over the tops of trees.

A loud whir pierced my ears. I leaned over the edge of my window. *What could have made that noise?* I saw nothing. I looked up glancing further out. *Had they found me?*

Something slightly came into view, blue light lit up the bottom of a black smoke cloud. My eyes followed the smoke, but it had no starting point.

Then I saw it, out of the smoke a small machine like that of an aircraft, glowing blue. I immediately noticed that this was a gyrocycle. It began swerving, zig-zaging from side to side, and then vanished almost as quickly. *What the-? Where did it go?*

I sat my book down next to me, the picture lay in the same place. Just as I looked back up, the gyrocycle reappeared, now only a couple feet in front of me. A man stood on top, the same stranger I had met before. Within a second he jumped off and landed on the windowsill.

In shock, I staggered to my feet, backing up. "Why are you in my room?" I burst out.

He put his hands up as to reassure me. "I am not here to hurt you."

"Why are you here?" I continued. So much confusion ran through my mind.

"You already know who I am." He jumped down from the windowsill and walked closer. *Why isn't he answering my questions?*

My heart was nearly jumping out of my chest. I stuttered slightly. "Aruno...the sky pirate?"

"The one and only." His stance was very egotistical.

"What do you want from me?!"

"Zath, I know you have great potential in the field of sky piracy." *Oh, dear.*

A lump formed in the back of my throat. "How do you know my name?"

He shook his head, "Doesn't matter."

The confidence in my words was not visible. "I don't steal from people."

Aruno let out a laugh. "We both know that's not true."

I rambled, "Stealing from people isn't what I like doing, I was forced to steal, I'm sorry I stole from your brother but," I stuttered. "I didn't mean it."

Aruno walked closer, "Look, I know that you started that riot, you could have put the entire country at risk of war."

"Orfeo would not start a war over something so small." I turned on my heel walking towards the door.

Aruno turned me around, locking the door behind me. "There is nothing stopping Orfeo's rage towards you now. If the Noble guards capture you they will throw you in jail or worse they would torture you." He stepped back. "There's two choices. One, stay here and get captured. Two, come with me, so I can keep you safe." His words felt calming, almost.

"What are the chances of them finding me?"

Aruno grinned slightly. "What were the chances of me finding you?"

I felt taken aback. He was right, I couldn't take the chances. The door knob jiggled slightly, "Zathena! I left my money on the bed!"

As I was about to speak he stopped me. "Why won't you unlock the door?" Then all was quiet as I heard her running off.

I tensed up as he looked straight in my eyes. "Zath, you asked me how I knew your name," With a grin he explained, "I know your Mother."

"No, you don't!" I exclaimed.

He spoke slowly, "Luna is on my airship." He pulled out a picture from his back pocket. It was Luna and Aruno standing beside each other wearing formal attire.

I turned my head as I stepped away from him. "My mother?" Tears stung my eyes, but never poured over.

Aruno smiled. "She wanted me to track you down. She needs to see you again Zath."

Just then the door behind me flew open, and in that instant Satomi was standing behind me with keys in her hand. Zilpher stood next to her, puzzled.

Satomi yelled in excitement, which startled me. "Oh my...you're Aruno!" I looked back at her, she continued. "I knew you would come one day!"

Aruno was smiling, but looked a little confused and taken aback. I felt like he got this sort of attention a lot, but maybe not this much.

"Uh, I'm glad you recognize who I am." Satomi just stood there staring at him with a huge smile.

Zilpher seemed annoyed still, "He cannot possibly know where our mother is Zathena; you can't believe this thief! His warrant is all over town!"

Aruno sounded apologetic. "None of them express who I truly am."

"They most certainly do," Satomi explained.

Aruno looked up, stroking his neck nervously "Uhh… thank you." he said.

"Zilpher, I still don't believe him, but he has a photo of our mother. Do you not see? He can help us find her!"

"This means you would be going to his airship. Sky pirates are murderers!"

"We have only killed a few Raqoian imperialist dogs; and only for the good of Queen and country!

"There is no Queen!" Zilpher objected irately.

"Uh… right, well I've never been a very political person" Aruno said, shrugging him off and walked towards me.

"What do you say Zath? Are you onboard?"

"I've dreamt of sky pirates my entire life." I smiled.

"Zilpher?" I walked over to him, "Do you realize what happened today? I started that riot after exiting from Orfeo's speech. I'm in danger if I stay here. Besides, I can take care of myself. I know how to handle people like Aruno." I said reassuringly.

Satomi gaped in disbelief, "You're the one that did that?! I can't believe this."

We heard screaming coming from downstairs. "They've found you. We don't have much time."

"I'll go with you, Aruno."

"If you need to leave, I'm coming with you. I've always wanted to be a sky pirate."

"That's fine, we need to go." Aruno demanded.

"Yay!" Satomi declared jumping up and down with joy.

"Satomi, I thought you didn't want to end up in jail." Zilpher said, puzzled.

She glared at him and said. "By the look of him, I don't think we will."

There was a louder commotion downstairs, and I could hear excited voices. The sound of plates clanking and hurried footsteps.

Aruno glanced at me out of the corner of his eye "Well... Looks like it's time to go" soon followed by the distinct sound of metal boots thundering against the rickety stairs.

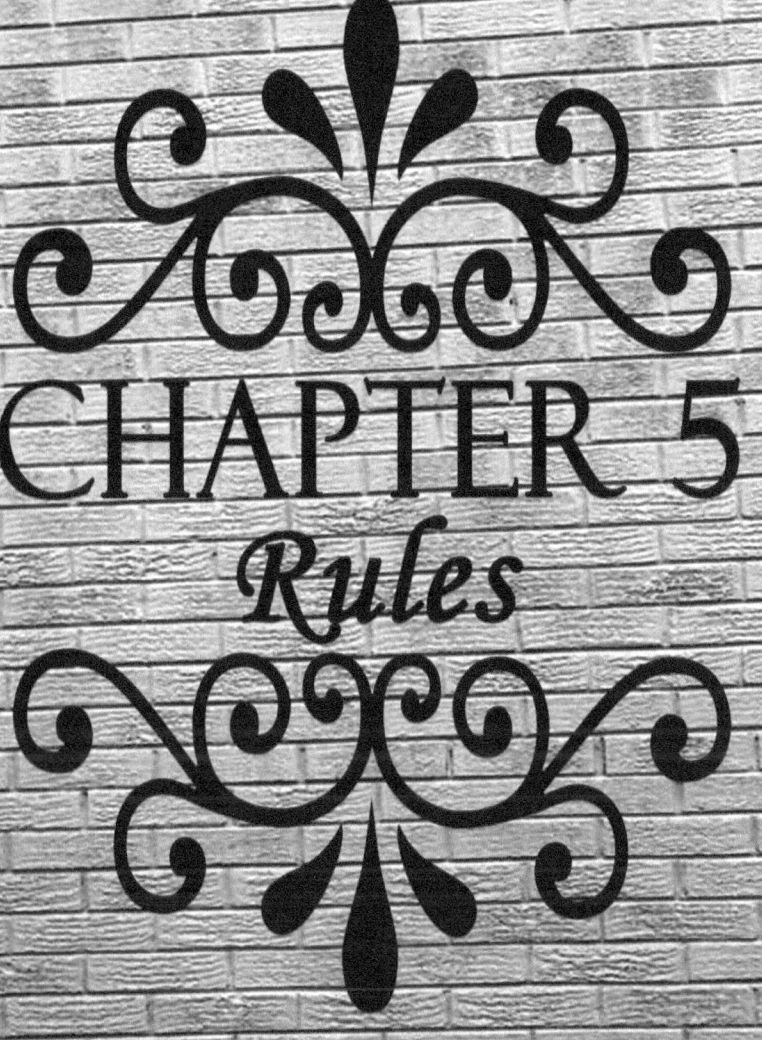

CHAPTER 5

Rules

*A*runo ran to the window clambered onto the windowsill and jumped the few feet through the abyss of open air to his hovering vehicle. He then lifted himself into the cockpit and flipped a latch. A part behind the pilot area slid back revealing a small seating area with four seats. I grabbed my satchel, and waited behind the others as they all filed through the window and clambered onto the ship as well. I found myself near the one free seat and put my massager bag under the seat there.

The vessel lit up as the steam engines behind our compartment warmed up to full flight mode, letting out a bright yellow glow. I was nervous because I had never flown before, but I was more excited to experience this. Then a blue light lit up around our seats and the vessel seemed to be evaporating and some odd looking steam was released which surrounded the ships exterior. The light seemed to be bending around us, making the air shimmer. The wonders of science, I mused.

I looked at the orphanage just before we set off. The few days I spent there, were the best I had since my mother left. It looked like I was never going to be able to return. And then as if to confirm that, soldiers smashed the doorway and spread across my room, searching for me. Our ship was hard to see with this advanced camouflage, but it still was noticeable if someone had spent a moment looking, as I did.

I didn't know if I could trust this sky pirate. Zilpher did have a point, Aruno could just be lying to get us to join him, though I'm not sure of what capturing us would achieve.

Before a soldier could notice our hovering form, we lifted up above the window and flew off into the twilight sky.

The view of the city from above was breathtaking. There was an interlinking wire network suspended above the city connected to towers which jutted from the ground below.

The city was dotted with areas that had great stone buildings and obelisks. These sections stood out with their overly gaudy and exquisite stylizing.

This I compared to humble dwellings of most of the city, them either being small and simply crafted or just hovels in expansive slums. The royal castle stood out among the slums, but held the same pleasant architecture. Vermyria's royal families rarely designed palatial. They wanted us to be equal, in a culturally vast country.

As the speed increased, and the air whipped around me and through my hair, things seemed clearer. I had escaped from this urban sprawl to a life that raveled greater than that; living with hundreds of sky pirates and Aruno the infamous.

A smile turned up the corners of my mouth. *Who knows what awaits me, maybe even a happy ending.*

We ascended through the clouds. I had wondered before what they were made of, and I was surprised to find nothing but foggy wet air.

As we emerged from the cloud layer, my ears popped and the site of the huge airship came into focus. It looked to be a beautiful old style ship. It had an actual water landing design. It had the feel of an old galleon from the age of sea travel. The ship was suspended bellow a large zeppelin shaped ridged canopy holding a separated envelope balloon design, shaped to the rigging, giving it the sleek zeppelin shape. Large sails extended from the sides of the back half canopy to capture the high velocity winds of the sky.

I saw a hanger which opened in the back of the ship, but instead of landing there, we descended over amid ship. As we approached the deck I could see no expense was spared at keeping the ship as extravagant as possible, the entrances had large designs made of expensive material like gold and silver.

Aruno landed on deck, and let the steam engines vent. He helped the passengers off with a flourish, trying to seem presentable. "Welcome to my in no way humble abode." Aruno bragged. "On my ship I have some rules. One doesn't open, touch, find, or locate the white door." He explained.

Satomi looked confused, and questioned "But why? What's behind the white door?"

Aruno replied "Nothing that concerns you. Don't make curiosity have more than cat's blood on its hands."

Satomi seemed to shrink a little with this slight threat. Zilpher whispered to her sarcastically, "I bet that's where he keeps his victims"

Aruno heard this comment and said, "You wouldn't want to be the one to find out." He then continued about his rule, "Also, don't go into my room under any circumstance. That's just wrong, a captain needs his space."

Satomi whined, "But what if you're dying-"

"That would most likely never happen." Aruno cut her off, "and you would be better off if you didn't ask so many questions!" he snapped. "The third rule is you can do whatever you feel like doing."

He paused and saw Satomi about to interject something

"I feel like one of you is going to say, 'But that brakes the first two rules'. These two rules are obviously the exception."

Satomi quietly fumed, "He doesn't have to be so mean."

Aruno opened the large door and ushered us inside saying "I hope I don't regret this" in a joking manner

CHAPTER 6

Tour

*S*atomi and I followed Aruno into the airship. Brass framework skylight windows rose about thirty feet above us in the shape of two ovals. The room was almost heart shaped with bronze framed windows, which bowed out at our sides and halted a little less than halfway across the room.

The room sunk below the first landing by a small set of stairs. The further end of the place was darkened by an upper floor walkway that wrapped around the walls and a stage at its center.

Filament contained within vacuum tube bulbs; were mounted on the bookshelves every few feet, giving the darker area an eerie glow. The area by the side windows held a cozy seating area with armchairs.

Mismatched, yet luxurious, expensive looking antique rugs lined the sitting area, and some sprawled down the aisles between bookcases.

"Wow," Satomi said in awe.

"Welcome to the Annabeth" Aruno said, smiling with pride. He tossed his gyrocycle keys to the nearest butler.

A young man walked up behind Aruno. He had short brown hair and a mechanical looking monocle. He was wearing a coat like a military leader with a short tasseled epaulette, tight leather pants, and tied boots up to the calves.

"Oh, new crew." The man talked with a strange, rounded accent with long vowels.

Aruno gestured toward the man. "This is Sir Jonny Baron." He gave a short bow when his name was mentioned. "He is our main weapons specialist aboard the Annabeth."

"G'day mate" We all exchanged our greetings. He looked around at the lot of us. "Now I knew Zathena was going to come here and likely with her friend; but who is this bloke?"

I jumped in, eager to answer the question. "This is Zilpher, my brother." Aruno looked over at Jonny with a grin; he glanced down snickering as he looked back over at us. "Oh, right your brother; that's understandable."

Satomi exclaimed, "What do you mean 'that's understandable?"

"It's nothing. I just always knew she had a brother." He stepped back. "Well, I'm off." he said, then proceeded upstairs.

"Let me give you the rest of the tour then." Aruno said with his back towards us. He walked down the stairs and across the lounge, past the bookcases, was handed a torch light by a new butler, and proceeded to a large double door at the other end of the room.

The door was a dark cherry wood; with very fine carvings all around the sides and on the square panels in the middle.

Aruno threw the doors open. He walked down the hall and stopped next to two closed doors, then turned to face us, "This is my room, on your right and Jonny's room on my right. The second rule applies here. "

I asked puzzled. "You said not to go in your room, you never mentioned Sir Jonny's."

Aruno looked at me flabbergasted. "Zathena, Don't be getting any ideas."

Zilpher attempted to stand up for me. "What ideas could she be possibly getting? She is a child."

Aruno stared Zilpher in the eyes. He then pivoted on his heel. "Well, on with the tour." He walked down past four doors. "Do not worry about these rooms, we will return to them later." He continued down the hallway and stopped in front of two airtight sealed doors.

Aruno started turning the wheel on the door. It popped from its airtight seal and loudly screeched as he pulled it.

We stepped into a room of foiled metal lined floors, and positioned about were large, ambiguous consoles with many bright glowing buttons. This room was like nothing I had ever seen before; nothing I ever knew was possible.

"What does all this do?" I said in amazement. Satomi rocked on her heels waiting for Aruno to reply.

"This is the command deck. All you need to know is that the crew knows what they are doing."

A few men were running around the bridge, torches in hand, plying wrenches to pipes, taping hoses, and ducking into small crawlspaces and racing down the stairs. They wore full body leather suits with sections belted together, and with long hoses connecting to the masks on their face, with small windowed holes for eyes.

Another group of men were pushing the buttons, turning dials. They wore dark vests, ties, and white buttoned up shirts; on the whole they looked very dignified. The butlers that I thought I saw earlier, where other sky pirates. *I'm finally starting to understand now.*

One particular vested man, short and heavyset with bulging eyes was making a scene, clanging a spanner against a strange bronze pole with levers, and rambling to himself loudly. "Keep it down, Melvin!" Aruno yelled over the commotion as he walked through the room. Melvin looked back at us, popping a large eyeball and smacking his lips together, then concentrated back on his work. I heard him grumble under his breath. "That irritates me more than my knickers."

I looked away frightened and whispered to Satomi, "What a creep!" Of course I didn't really mean it, well maybe I did, but only because at the time I didn't really know him well.

Aruno maneuvered over large rubber hoses on the floor, and stopped in front of a large, dome-like window at the ship's bow. "And this is the helm. The crown of the whole girl." Aruno held his torch over a great and dark wooden wheel, with great etchings and gold overlay. "Can't all be modern. This wheel's off an ancient vessel, from days when pirates preferred the sea instead of the sky. From the very treasury of the Raqoian royal family. Nicked it myself." He said with pride while caressing the wheel. One of the machinists in the masks ran over to us and stood at attention, his leather helmet was a patchwork of red and brown, tight to his face and the tiny glass eye-windows fogged up as he spoke "Sir, preparations are almost finished. We'll be ready to roll silent again before the moon rises on high. As soon as you wrap things up here?"

Aruno looked at the lad sharply before he turned his gaze back to us.

"Let's continue on the tour then." We all turned around, ready to leave. "Go through this door." The door was a dark grey with heavy set cogs along the middle. When Aruno turned the door handle the cogs rotated around until a loud clank was heard. The door opened by itself then revealing a galley with prep tables.

Aruno gestured us inside speaking. "Come on, get out of their way." We all walked inside the kitchen.

Zilpher inquired, "What I don't understand is, why the kitchen is so close to the command deck?"

Aruno shut the door behind us, vexed at the question. He looked toward Zilpher, smiling. I sensed sarcasm in his voice as he spoke. "Well Zilpher, I fly the ship drunk sometimes."

"That makes me feel safe." Zilpher was irked. Satomi and I laughed in unison. I was really starting to enjoy with the idea of being a sky pirate. Aruno soon told me that a boiler powered the electrical generator and was used to filter water for drinking along with heating the oven.

"The entire airship is powered by steam?" I asked surprised. He replied with the nod of his head. I felt so amazed! I heard most airships were powered by fossil fuels.

Aruno pointed to two golden painted doors in the back of the kitchen. "Those doors lead to the mess hall." He smiled. "You girls will have to set the tables in the morning and wash dishes during the day."

"Why? I want to become an adventurer!" Satomi asked curiously. "Plus, back in the orphanage everyone had to wash their own dishes most days."

"Well, I was going to keep this a surprise..." His voice held with anticipation. "Zilpher is starting his war training tomorrow," Zilpher smiled with confidence, "and since you girls will be lounging around most of the day doing nothing, you need to help out."

I nodded. "We would be happy to help." I looked at Satomi to reassure her. "It will be fun."

We exited through the side doors leading into the hallway once more. Light from a lantern's flame flickered across the walls. "We meet upstairs at 0600 in the War Training room to receive assignments, posted by yours truly." He held a grin. "Sir Jonny will lead you there in the morning."

We proceeded to walk down the corridor. We halted at the two rooms we had earlier walked past. Aruno slowly opened the door revealing a vintage royal en suite equipped with two beds.

One rose high, with deep cherry wood bedstead frames and headboard, and a pink frilled drapery which trailed to the floor. In front, rested a red textile fainting sofa and accompanying that; a Pugin table.

The other bed, a half tester, had a rod iron frame with intricate baubles fixed in its barred headboard. In front was a purple Queen Anne sofa, equipped with a black gold trimmed Louis xiv-style chair and footrest.

The baronial room had a light wooden floor decorated with a large rug appointed in the middle. On top of that stood at two feet tall one and-a-half feet wide rustic Wardian case on a stand, ferns flourished the inside. Three portholes decorated the walls, moonlight filling most of the room.

Lamps hung on the wall, cascading several shadows. A marble top washstand stood by the far west wall. On the far south, next to where we stood, an opened large winged wardrobe stuck out of the wall.

Tall shelves covered the east wall, adorned with many different sizes of books.

"This is where you girls will be staying," His grin stayed. "Hope you like it."

"I love it! It is so splendid!" Satomi was nearly jumping out of her socks.

"Did you always have this room, decorated like this?" I stood flabbergasted from excitement.

Aruno handed us the keys to the room. "Well, I have been acquiring things over the years." He quickly changed the subject. "Zilpher," He hesitated his gaze from us. "You will be staying across the hall. I would let you stay in the sleeping quarters but the crew doesn't take a liking to," His eyebrow went up, "New... people." *What is he talking about?* We followed Aruno as he walked across the hall.

The door across from ours was adorned with solid gold lettering in the Raqoian language, which I did not find out, mind you; until later that night.

Zilpher had a slight twisted face when he saw the markings. Come to think of it, how could he understand Raqoian from earlier today? These thoughts soon passed when I realized he had to have learned it from secondary schooling.

To the fore side of the room there was a large porthole window with gold trim, filling the room with intense moonlight. At the far east wall, facing center, stood a luxurious sleigh bed with a very welcoming double down comforter.

In front of which lay a gold, pine coffer. A gentleman's washstand was present on the opposite wall; marble top and inlaid gold carvings on its cabinet doors. In the middle of the floor, a crimson red Victorian sofa with end tables on either side.

Next to the end tables were winged back chairs facing each other. In the middle lay a wide tea table on top of a luxurious red, black, and gold rug.

To the west side of the room a simple wardrobe, forward of that a crimson ladder back tête-à-tête with gold trim.

"Whose room was this originally?" Zilpher asked absentmindedly.

"That should not concern you. Whoever had been here last is gone now."

Suddenly the room was filled with a long, howling shriek from the air ducts. Aruno looked anxious and confused. "I'll..." He hesitated. "Be right back." He walked off in a short haste.

We stood in a circle, facing each other. "What do you think that was?" Satomi asked concerned, fear filled her eyes.

"It's really hard telling."

"Wait, Zilpher, can you read the door's plaque?" I needed to rephrase, being Vermyrian and able to read Raqoian is sometimes considered an insult to some people. "I am just assuming, because I overheard you talking with that guard."

"I can. Also, Aruno's reaction to my question makes me suspicious."

Satomi anxiously asked, "Zilpher, what does it say?"

"It reads Kazuhiko Mirashikari."

I jumped, "Do you mean the prince of Raqoia?"

"Of course, he went missing about three years ago."

"You don't think he..." I paused, and continued with a whisper, "killed him, do you?"

"Aruno would never do such a thing!" Satomi whispered indignantly. "He couldn't even steal from others. He only steals back what belongs to him."

"How did you acquire this knowledge, Satomi?" Zilpher asked knowingly.

She grabbed at my nap sack, and pulled out a book "This book! It's about famous sky pirates."

"Satomi, that's small evidence only found in a book."

"How did you know I had that?" I grabbed the book back from Satomi. "Did you read it? I don't like it with other people take my belongings. This belonged to my mother."

"Sorry Zathena," Satomi said apologetically, "I didn't think about where you got it, I just really like reading about airships and stuff."

"It's okay," I laughed, "plus, Zilpher is telling the truth." I added sarcastically, "I am certain that everything Aruno sees belongs to him."

Without my knowing, Aruno appeared behind me. "That's normally the rule." I jumped in surprise. "Except, I can't exactly keep everything I've stolen, my crew deserves most of it. Don't you think?"

"I uh..." I said, taken aback.

He laughed loudly, "Of course, I wouldn't actually steal from my own crew." He glanced at the clock on the wall, "Well, time for you girls to go to bed, work starts at 0400."

Aruno started walking to his door.

"Aruno wait!" I ran after him as he stopped. "You still haven't told me." He turned around as I paused. "Where's my mother?"

"Oh, your mother?" He smirked, "You see, I don't actually know where she is. The day I met her, she was working at a Raqs sharqi cabaret."

My heart fell out of my chest. I have never felt so naive. I felt like every inch of my body was fighting back the urge to run out on deck and jump overboard. My instinctive action was to defend my mother.

"My mother would never do such a thing! She was a good modest woman! You self righteous git!" I yelled enraged.

"Next time, listen to your brother." He calmly stated before he slammed his bedroom door behind him.

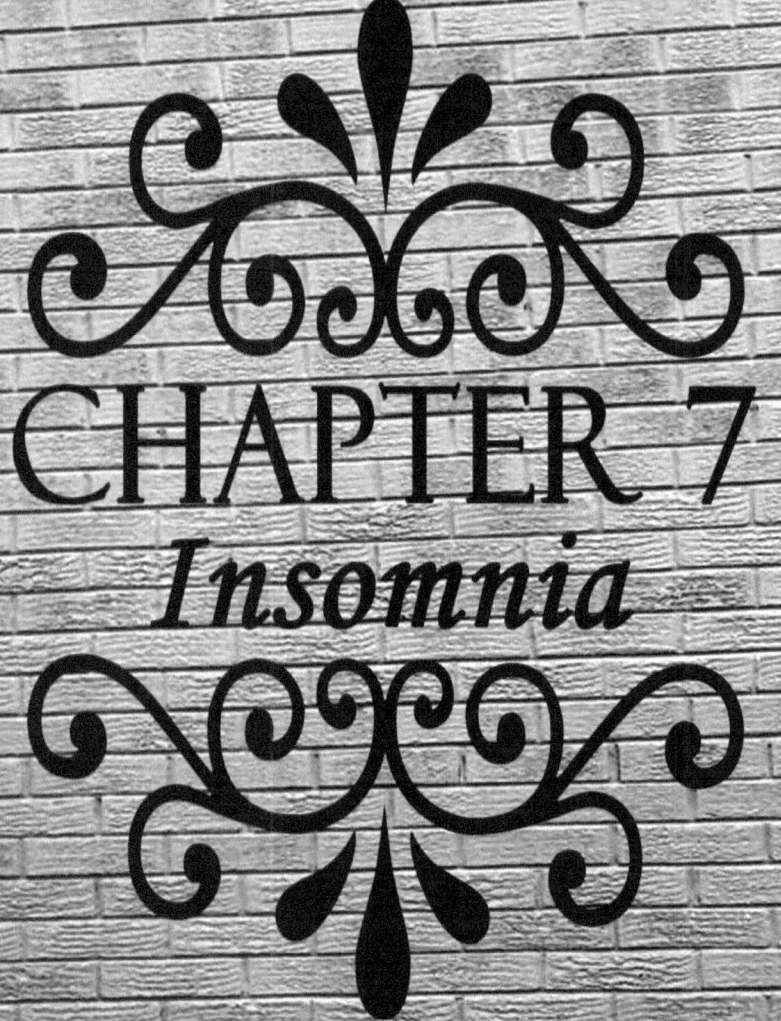

CHAPTER 7
Insomnia

I could feel a lump form in the back of my throat. Hot tears collected in my eyes. I held the tears back trying to keep my composure.

I turned around, Zilpher stood there staring at me not entirely sure of what to say. I started walking back slowly to my bedroom. "He probably didn't mean it in that way." Satomi reassured.

I was enraged. *Oh really! Then why was I brought here?* I felt completely alone. Satomi believed Aruno exaggerated. Zilpher wouldn't even look at me. He was right about Aruno, and I felt like I was going to die with this never ending guilt.

As I moved closer to my door, tears just about flooded over. Zilpher grabbed my arm, pulling me close, embracing me. "Zathena, everything will be fine, I promise."

Holding back my tears was no longer a priority to me. I felt secure in his arms, but I pushed him away. "I need to go..." I quickly ran to my room.

I threw open the door to the en suite's bathroom. The room was plainly tiled white, with one white claw foot tub with a veil falling around the edges. Looking back in the mirror was a girl covered with running makeup.

The white porcelain sink was adorned with dimly glowing bulbs of light. On a stand next to the sink laid a neatly folded towel. I layered it with the bar of soap and lifted the towel to my soft skin, wiping away my tears along with the makeup from the day before. Drying my face with the other side of the towel, I noticed something strange.

Lifting it from my skin I noticed the towel was embroidered on one side with a name in gold, Zathena.

I jumped startled, throwing the towel in the sink. The letters were written in Vermyrian, they looked so strange to me. They gave me an almost eerie feeling. *Why would that be in there?*

I left the bathroom still in shock, and sat on my Queen Anne sofa, in a daze of confusion.

I heard a knock at the door. Zilpher called out, "I need to talk to you. Can I come in?" Him talking to me would make me feel better, but letting him see me cry over something, so naive?

"Uh, ok." I whispered, hoping he could not hear me.

Zilpher let himself in. "Are you okay?"

"I am fine." My voice seemed a bit shaky.

He sat near me. "Zath, if you aren't fine you should tell me."

I looked down at my hands rested in my lap. "I'm sorry I should have listened to you." I looked back at him. "Why would Aruno lie to us?"

"I think he must be looking for our mother, but not for you."

"What do you mean?"

"I don't know what his motives are but, if you're here and Mother is looking for you, he has the upper hand."

I felt so disgusted at the thought of being used. "We need to get out of here…"

"I know you want to leave, but we can't yet. You and I'd have to plan ahead."

"And Satomi." He smiled at my reminder. I knew nothing horrible could happen if he were here. *Even though he didn't want to adventure here, I'm glad he came along with me.*

Before I was entirely finished with what I was going to say, Zilpher ended the conversation. "I'll talk with you tomorrow morning." I had too many questions I wanted to ask him.

"Alright," I grinned back. "See you." I never wanted him to leave when he did.

After Zilpher left, I changed into my nightgown. It was laced white ruffled and long with the back trailing the floor. More ruffles laid around the collar trimmed with gold.

Soon after, Satomi ran into the room holding a small black porcelain bowl. Excitement took over her appearance. I turned my attention to her. "Where did you get that?"

"They have an ice cream parlor here!"

"An entire room, all devoted to ice cream?"

"Yes! Needless to say, I screamed." She giggled with excitement.

"Are you sure that's what they usually serve there?"

"Uh, well, no. You see, they wouldn't serve me anything else."

"I see." Laughter broke out in the room amongst us.

I became serious. "You better give me some of that."

*   *   *   *   *

It was hard for me to sleep that night. The constant irritation of the previous events kept creeping back inside my mind. What would Aruno want in finding my mother? I could not keep my mind wondering, my eyelids became heavy, and I soon found myself asleep.

The ship came alive, jolting forward, with yelps of cheers. I awoke suddenly, hearing a steam valve screeching near the vents. I sat up. The ship movements were different to me, almost causing me to feel sick. After a couple minutes however, it felt normal. I stumbled as I stood up, and walked out the door like a drunkard.

Loud blaring howls like the ones I heard just hours before, echoed in my ears. I caught my balance. *Where could that be coming from?*

I started walking to Zilpher's room, contemplating on whether or not I should attempt to awaken him. I would have felt horrible to make him get up, knowing that he had training in the morning, so I walked away.

I walked down the hallway to the main library entrance. The room felt cold, and the strange lights had grown dim. I sauntered along a few feet and the soft faint noise grew louder.

As I glided past a space between the books, I caught a glimpse of someone who sat in a nearby wingback chair. I quickly hid back behind the books and peered around into the opening. He was gone; maybe I was just seeing things in my tired state.

"What are you doing awake?" I gasped as I turned around. Sir Jonny stood at attention, with his lips creased into a smirking grin.

"I could ask the same about you." I said, shaken but still trying to portray confidence under Jonny's piercing stare.

"I'm in charge of the night shift."

"What does one do while in charge of the night shift?" He smirked once more. "You're avoiding my question."

"It's hard for me to sleep."

"Not use to the turbulence?"

"Yea, but I'm also not use to hearing people scream in the middle of the night!"

"Whatever do you mean?"

"Can you..." I pondered my question. "Not hear it?"

He looked up, confused. "Are you sure you're not hearing the steam valves. Or are airship's foreign to you?" I sensed sardonic within his voice and it irritated me.

"No, I know of airships well!" I sounded maddening, so I attempted calming myself. "I hear someone screaming I swear."

"Where do you hear it coming from?"

"It's coming from upstairs."

He smiled, "would you like to accompany me while I figure out where this noise is coming from?"

Not with you anyone but you.

I nervously laughed. "Uhh… Ok."

We went around to the long, narrow staircase near the entrance lounge. This walk space was extremely tight, almost it made me feel indispose. The railings were gothic sculpted cast iron and as tall as I. Felt almost a little worried the thing might collapse, and so I moved up slowly.

"What's the matter?" Jonny asked, in front of me.

"This staircase is awkward." I laughed again.

"Aruno's a bit particular on the design of this place. He likes everything to be new as can be. I don't get why. It's not like the pirates around here care one bit for being civil. Maybe it just reminds the Captain of his former home…"

"I'm surprised something this fancy and impractical is desirable for an airship."

"Quite. Still, it's elegant," he paused, "You should see Melvin try to get up here."

I laughed a little, but then halted as we reached the top of the stairs. The entire second floor was just as elaborate as the last. Below the massive windows, a giant chandelier held up with ropes etched in gold, and strung up like a spider web, was suspended up over a small brown glossy stage.

The front of the stage had railings. Around one corner of the room, near the end of the prolonged window, rested small dining tables huddled around a wide bar. Or what Satomi called an "ice cream parlor". I laughed at the thought.

Sir Jonny halted and looked back at me. "Have you been swallowing nitrous oxide?"

"Have I been... what?"
He laughed a little, "It seems it's contagious." With that we continued walking ahead.

Large mats lined the right side of the stage; mechanical exercise machines lined the far walls.

I could hear a low screeching groan; he turned back around to face me. "Is that what you were referring to?" I nodded.

He let out a laugh. "That's nothing, I promise." We walked across the training room and down a long hallway, just past the bar.

I started to smell a faint musty smell; I heard the shrieks of steam popping from rusty pipes. I looked down at the floor, which had been varnished but was now deteriorated and scuffed.

I looked up, practically gagging at the heavy, musty smell as we reached the door at the end of the hall. It was dirty, with smut around the frame.

Jonny shouldered the heavy door open, revealing a soot covered room, with heavy iron machinery spewing flame and carts of coal every few feet. There were a few grimy faced, soot covered workers shoveling coal and adjusting levers.

"See, no worries. Just some vents making noises."

"No. I heard something... more human."

"Right then, well, your ears can fool you."

I sighed "You're probably right."

But out of all the darkness in the room, behind cables and chains, there was a narrow white door covered in soot.

Jonny looked down at me, noticing my interest in the matter. "We should get moving; we don't want to be in the way." I looked behind me at the white door as he rushed me out of the room.

We walked through the upper corridor, moonlight cast over the room, which Jonny looked up at, nodded and remarked, "Four am." He turned his head over toward the bar. "There's something about the bartender on this shift I just take a liking to, although I don't quite know what it is."

I followed him toward the bar which was located on the other side of the stairs. A woman stood behind the bar, pouring liquor in a glass for an old gentlemen. His head drooped over his food unable to tactfully grab the glass in a normal effort.

Jonny rested his arm on the bar table. "Ello, Donna, beautiful night, isn't it?" The women, now known as Donna looked like a real mixologist. Her low waist high slit skirt held loosely with a leather belt, which revealed her slender legs. Her loose white blouse was held tight with a waist cincher.

Holding a towel in one hand, she flung it as she spoke. "Look here," She nodded toward me, "save it for your pirate friend." She slapped it on the table, leaving it there.

Jonny raised an eyebrow. "You know-*you* could be my pirate friend."

"Nah, I don't think so, I already have one of my own."

He further smiled leaning toward her. "Oh? Do- *tell*."

He had noticed her intentions before she moved; within an instant she pulled a dagger from her back pocket, stabbing the table where his hand once laid. I felt like this happened on a regular basis. "I'll come back when you're in a better mood lassie."

We proceeded to walk down the stairs then; he turned to smile at me. "She can't resist me."

I sarcastically remarked, "Oh right, that's the vibe I got."

As we reached the library, Jonny pulled out a book from the nearest shelf. He sat over by the seating area near the side windows, gesturing me to sit near him.

As I did, he examined the book he found. It was gray, the front faded it could not be recognized. He smiled and handed it to me. The cover felt rough, with small indented silhouettes on the cover.

"When I first got here I was uncomfortable. I had trouble getting to sleep and I missed my home. This book well reminded me of my past." He smiled after reminded of his memories. "I read it when I couldn't sleep." He handed me the book, "Keep it, it should help you sleep. Maybe now you can stop bothering me." He quipped with a smile.

"Thank you." I smiled back.

"It's nearly time for the morning shift."

"I will leave soon." I couldn't get my mind off of the white door and how odd Sir Jonny had acted once I noticed it. I changed the subject. "Jonny, what's behind the white door?"

I nettled at his nerves, although he wasn't showing it. "That is a question you shouldn't be asking."

"Is it possibly a generator room?"

He looked antagonized from my questions as he sat silenced. I could hear someone walking behind us, coming from the barrack. A man turned the corner from around the bookcases.

He was wearing a tight, black jacket with vest and tie. His pants hung a bit low with a gun holster. His hair was messy, and he wore one metal eye patch. His stare held menacingly. He spoke to Jonny, "I'm here to relieve you."

"I am aware."

He nodded at Jonny. "Who is this young lady?" he said, keeping his stare.

"She's one of our new recruits."

"Are you positive?" He let out a laugh.

"I am. It's Aruno's orders."

"That sounds just about right of him." He grinned.

What was that supposed to mean? I felt incredibly uncomfortable.

"Right." Jonny stood up about to leave.

"You're leaving?" I asked curtly. I felt uncomfortable as it was.

"There are other things that need my attention. And Avner here needs to start working." He smiled at me before he left.

I tried to ignore the stranger that stood before me.

"Do you really want to know what's behind the white door?" His grin stayed. He reached behind him to pull something out of his back pocket. "There is something you really need to see."

I stood up. "What?"

He handed me a small black key. It felt cold in my hand.

"The key to the White room is in Aruno's bedroom. It's in his desk; first drawer." He looked around frantic. "You did not hear this from me. It's not safe to go there. Make sure you are not seen nor followed."

I hid the key gently in my hand. "I don't think this would be a good idea."

"There are secrets on this ship. Some too frightening to find out, but this one is important." He stared at me imposingly.

"But, why is it important to me?"

"If you go, you will find out." He walked past me, and slipped behind a bookshelf.

*   *   *   *   *

As I walked to my bedroom I thought about whether or not I should actually go through with it. I really did not see why I had to be on the ship, and; *it would be interesting to find out what Aruno could be hiding.*

Zilpher walked out of his bedroom and stood in the hallway. "Hello…" He seemed confused. "Do you never sleep?"

"There's something I need to tell you."

"What might that be?" I barged through the door of his bedroom, as he followed behind.

"The white door."

He shut his door behind him. "What about the white door?"

"Where do you think it leads to?"

"I was just thinking about that; I don't have the slightest idea."

"When I asked Sir Jonny, he completely ignored me. Why would they need to keep the door a secret? Maybe it has something to do with us."

"Of course they are hiding something from us. Everyone has their kept secrets and they do seem very dismissive about it." He looked away from me, "This may even be more impossible to uncover then I thought."

"Well I know how we can."

I handed the key the stranger gave me, to Zilpher who then studied it closely. "This is the key to Aruno's room."

"How did you know that?"

He smiled at me. "What do you plan on doing?"

"The key to the white door is in Aruno's room." Zilpher appeared to be shocked. "I have his key."

He handed the key back to me. "This is dangerous. You just can't walk into Aruno's room unnoticed without him finding out. He is an infamous sky pirate, nothing can get past him. We could get thrown overboard for insubordination."

"We have nothing to lose."

"We have each other."

"*And* Satomi." I added.

"Of course. Listen, If you really want to go through with this, I can distract Sir Jonny; but I don't want you going alone. Ask Satomi maybe she would like to go with you."

"I'll talk to her." I hid the key again as I walked out of his room.

I walked back in my room, finding Satomi still asleep. I decided to get a few more hours of sleep in before woken up again. Instead I could only sleep for a couple of minutes, and then I woke back up.

I walked near the wardrobe and changed into something nice I found. It was tight like a corset, and puffy with ruffles at the bottom with some trail. White lace draped around the front. It felt silky, and wasn't the slightest bit heavy. There was a table next to the wardrobes with small satchel bags.

The one nearest to me was brown; I picked it up and draped it around my shoulder.

Satomi woke up in a daze. "Why are you up so early?"

I shrugged. "Couldn't sleep."

"I'm so sorry." She said as she sat up wiping her eyes.

"Satomi, get dressed." She stood up and walked to her side of the wardrobe.

"Oh, I forgot we had chores."

"Yea, but I have other plans."

"Why? Is this because of yesterday?"

"Absolutely. I'm not going to perform demeaning chores for some infamous fool. I've been reading about him for years. This is one thing never recorded. I need to figure out what's so special about this white door and why the prince's name is written on the plaque."

Satomi looked flabbergasted. "You're right, even the basic plans of the Annabeth from officials have nothing recorded about this special door."

"I have the key to Aruno's room, I know where to find the key to the white door. Do you want to come with me?"

"We shouldn't really do that. We're going to get thrown off the ship. You know how much I longed to be here."

"I honestly never knew that. You told me not to touch your books remember? Oh well; he's hiding something from me, and I think this might have something to do with my mom."

"But... I don't think we should look through his personal belongings. What if he finds out?"

"Satomi; personal— *belongings*." I repeated.

She thought about it for a minute and as if it made up her mind, "Okay, I'm in."

CHAPTER 8

The White Door

*W*e walked hurriedly down the hall to Aruno's room.

"Do you know if he's in his room?" Satomi asked.

"I have no clue."

"Well, only one way to find out."

Coming up to the door I paused, and made my mind up on whether to knock or not. I could hear Aruno's leather combat boots shuffling toward us. Satomi backed up a little, as he slowly opened the door.

Aruno stood blocking the doorway. He wore a long sleeve white shirt rolled up to his elbow. With a deep brown vest over top with a red puff tie. His black pants held up with many belts.

I tried to see into his room but I couldn't. He studied the both of us, intrigued. "Yes?"

"We are on our way to the galley." I said, very arid. I was seriously hoping he was at the command deck already.

"I'm headed that way now," he smiled. "Did you need anything?"

Satomi replied, "I just wanted to see you before we went to set the tables…"

"Oh, well, I'm glad you came to see me." He seemed to have noticed me glowering at him. He stepped out of his room, closing the door behind him.

"Did you sleep well?" He asked Satomi smiling.

"I uh… yea, it was difficult, but I managed to sleep alright." Satomi responded.

I rolled my eyes, irritated. Aruno and Satomi started walking down the corridor to the dining hall. I followed closely behind as they had their own separate conversation, forgetting my existence. *I can't believe this.*

"All you need to do is set the tables. The crew can take care of the rest."

"That's fine. I love it here and I would like to help in any way." Satomi agreed with a smile. Aruno ignored my presence had started to seriously annoy me. He seemed cowardly to not even address what he had said about my mother yesterday.

We entered the brightly lit dining hall, and the wooden chairs were stacked on the long tables. Five large cupboards were opened in the far back.

"Melvin will tell you how we like our tables set, so check in with him." Aruno exited into the kitchen.

"Satomi, did you notice how he completely avoided eye contact with me?"

"Ye-"

Satomi was cut off when the far door behind her quickly opened. Aruno stood outside the galley. "Well? We don't have all day." Satomi and I walked towards Aruno.

Satomi half laughed when she saw Melvin, who wore a grimy apron, hair net and rubber gloves pulled up to his elbow. He looked irritated.

Aruno nodded at him and entered the command deck. Melvin smiled at us which made him seem not so bad, he was possibly happy to see us.

"How are you doing?" He was mixing batter in a bowl.

I spoke for Satomi. "We are fine."

"Here to help set the tables?" He stopped what he was doing and grabbed a plate and silverware. He set the plate on the metal prep table and put the fork and knife next to each other on the right of the plate.

Followed by, laying the spoon to the left. "The fork on the right; next goes the knife; spoon to the left; this is what's best. Yah got that?" I fumbled as he handed me the silverware causing me to drop the fork. "You're already over cookin' my grits." He stated while glaring at me.

"But, I'm not cooking grits." I said confused. Satomi snickered to herself.

He snarled. "It was a metaphor."

Satomi and I left going to the dining hall. We walked to the back table, and as Satomi put down a couple chairs, I set a table.

"Uh, I think we should leave now and get it over with." I whispered.

"Sure, let's go." Satomi agreed.

We slipped out of the dining hall, swiftly walking through the hallway. We stopped at the captain's quarters. Adrenaline rushed through my veins. As I shook I put the key in its lock. The lock turned with a satisfying clink.

I hesitated against the door, but Satomi pushed it open quickly and raced in. Satomi gestured for me to hurry into the room with her.

The room was a vintage en suite with varnished oak and golden embroidery on the walls. Extended angled windows lined the far back walls. In front of which, a large mahogany desk with strangely detailed Raqoian embroidered a complex array of drawers and hidden compartments.

On the side of the room was his very own massive steam fed cannons extending outside. A circular wooden table sat in the middle of the room covered with several bottles of rum, grog, gin, and whiskey, which was surrounded by two leather wingback chairs, with leather footstools. Rapiers, katanas, and scimitars lined the far left wall behind a great detailed black full tester bed creating a headboard.

I ran over to his desk knowing I only had a couple of minutes to retrieve the key; Aruno could walk in at anytime. The first drawer on the desk was labeled in Raqoian. As

I pulled it open three small gold keys rested inside. I stole all three keys stuffing them into my satchel bag. We heard someone walking outside the room.

Satomi jumped up walking to the door. She peered outside. "We need to hurry."

"Right."

I ran out the door, Satomi had opened. I looked behind me and calmly walked to the lobby with her at my side. Walking into the lobby I saw that the strange man, Avner, from earlier was surrounded by at least twenty other men. He was giving out orders left and right, to fetch water or to swab the deck. Satomi and I walked to the stairs and slowly made our way up them.

On the second floor, on the other side of the room, Jonny stood with his back to us. We crouched low to the floor behind a railing, separating us from the stage and training corridor.

The sun had not risen over the elongated windows and the second floor was covered by the absent sun's yellow light. As we crept closer to the training mats, we could over hear Sir Jonny explaining Zilpher's training. "And you need to make sure that your weight is on your rear leg. That's the best way to keep stable in a fight."

Zilpher was leaning on a wooden scimitar, definitely heavy enough to knock a man out cold. He gazed at Jonny and seemed to be utterly bored. He kept lolling in the same pose.

Jonny, who didn't seem to notice Zilpher's bemusement at his explanation, was miming fencing moves with an invisible partner "Parry... Riposte!" Zilpher turned to Jonny "Alright, are we ready to get started?"
"If you think you're above my instruction, I'll have to demonstrate through humiliation. Let's go." Zilpher stood upright and assumed a fighting pose.

We snuck to the boiler room constantly looking over our shoulders, making sure no one was following us.

The door was still unclean, oily handprints covered the bronze door handle. The door was warped into the frame. "It won't budge." I managed to whisper. The screeching steam pipes grew louder. Satomi kicked the door, ajar. We slipped in shutting it behind us.

The workers seemed to only half notice us. Their bodies grimed with soot. Most of them had almond shaped eyes like that of Raqoians. A couple of them looked over at us, confused. While most just continued working, too busy to bother with new recruits.

Dodging carts, loose wires, and pipes billowing hot steam, Satomi and I maneuvered our way to the back of the room.

When we reached the white door, I pulled out all three gold keys. I looked through them. The first key embroidered with a Vermyrian symbol for humility, a mouse. I slipped it into the lock. I tried to turn the key but it was restricted from going any farther.

The second key was embroidered with the Yavanhyoto symbol for life a dragon, which its body was the key itself. I attempted to put the key in the lock, but the key wouldn't even fit.

The third key was the Raqoian seal a crow. Crows were the symbol for secrets. I remembered learning these things from a book my father read to me when I was little. I slipped the key into the lock. My heart filled with doubt. The key wouldn't turn.

A red light turned on and suddenly the door edged its way open. Satomi and I looked at each other with confused expressions. My heart pounded.

"Maybe we shouldn't do this..." Satomi muttered breathlessly. She trembled as she looked behind her.

"But we need to." I reassured.

I stepped through the doorway, the floor felt rough under my feet, and it was too dark to really see. The walls were barely illuminated by one small candle's light. On the opposite wall was an unlit bronze plated lantern.

I lifted it off the wall, and lit it with the candle. The door behind us slowly closed shut with a blood curdling squeal.

Looking at the floor I noticed I was standing on a rusted steel grated platform. A spiral staircase rested on the end of the catwalk. As I stepped foot on the staircase, we heard a ferocious, distorted growling. It echoed in the hollow dark. Satomi's eyes widened with fear. "I'm not going any further."

I exclaimed "Satomi?"

"If Aruno told us not to go; there has to be a reason for it."

I sighed. "Okay, but if you hear anything, please come find me."

I started walking down the long staircase, engulfed in darkness. The light from my lantern, created a safe haven from the black darkness. The growling became more definite, rattling my eardrums. The light from below seemed eerie and uncertain. My body felt colder with each step downward. The stairs felt like they went on forever and as the ground underneath my feet seemed to slip away, the closer my mind came to understanding what true fear was. Fog loomed around my ankles, then wrapped around my torso, then soon my entire body.

I finally reached the floor, swaying with dizziness. A foul stench stung my nose and grabbed at my senses. I held my lantern outward to find my surroundings.

The once white painted walls were peeling away. The floor was covered in unidentifiable liquid. Some parts of the walls were covered in a green molded moss. Several rusty sliding doors with small windows were spaced apart on both sides of the corridor.

One of the doors shook slightly as I walked by it, causing me to jump. I walked faster down the hallway. Candles spatially placed on the walls had melted to piles of wax.

I suddenly heard a high pitched crank and buzz sound down the hall. I slowed my pace as my heart filled with fear. The knot in my gut grew. *This was a horrible mistake.*

I stopped more than halfway down the hall. I slowly turned around, about to leave, then I started hearing clanging noises and dragged sounds.

The door next to me was open, revealing iron bars held tight with a lock. I walked toward it, my curiosity took over. I could vaguely see someone standing with his face in the corner.

He was tall, with lanky long skinny arms. His spine bulged about his gray bare back. His thighs were as slender as his arms. He turned around suddenly, fear withheld in his eyes. His loose structured face was sunken in, and distorted.

He jolted his head from one side to the other, twitching his neck as he digitigrades closer to the bars. One dead foot dragged behind him.

"I wouldn't go near him if I were you." His mouth wasn't moving, but I thought for sure the voice was coming from it.

As I started to back away, the skeleton of a man attacked the steel bars baring his teeth, which were unlike those of a human's.

He had several different rows of scattered about teeth. His eyes were black pools of nothingness. I screamed, startled and dropped my lantern. "Step away from the bars and you will be fine." My eyes were starting to water. "You're not going to get hurt, I promise."

I realized the voice wasn't coming from the creature, so I looked around the hall, still in fear. "Where are you?" I said shaking.

"Turn around."

I turned around and walked closer to the voice. Behind the metal bars, I noticed a cell fit for a king; at least a king in captivity. There was an elegant roll top writing desk with a fine leather surface, a chesterfield loveseat, and a regency-style bed.

He walked into the glow of my lantern. I felt startled when I saw him. His left eye was mechanically scarred, etches of clockwork intertwined within his retina. On the left side of his face, spread out around his temple, was red pus mixed with his charcoal burned skin that glistened in the light. His hair was black and cut short on one side. He looked similar to Orfeo, but with softer toned features. His shirt and pants were mangled and tore.

"You shouldn't be wandering around down here." He said intently.

"I've been warned."

"Heed the warnings; this isn't fog. You really need to leave this place."

I looked around, "Why? And what do you mean?"

"This place is where nightmares come alive, from the darkest corners of imagination."

Could this be him? "Who are you?" He looked so familiar.

"I'm sure you can guess." The room across from mine belonged to the prince. Orfeo always spoke of his brother, and the pain his kidnapping brought. The noblemen of Raqoia posted fliers about him everywhere.

"Your... highness?"

He didn't answer, but smiled.

"My name is Zathena -"

He spoke over me, "I already know who you are."

My eyes widened. "Oh." *That's kind of creepy.* "If you don't mind me asking, why are you here?"

He half looked away, "Aruno put me here, and it's quite a long story. What are you doing down here?"

"Aruno told me my mother was on this airship. I need to find her."

He looked down, "It's been ages since I have seen her."

"You knew my mother?" I exclaimed.

"Absolutely," He smiled. "She lived on the airship for a while."

"Yesterday I asked Aruno where she was, he told me he met her once at a Raqs sharqi cabaret!"
Kazuhiko laughed. "Never trust a sky pirate."

Footsteps were heard walking our way. A tall bald man wearing goggles, a long white lab coat, black pants and dark rubber gloves descended down the hallway, pushing a human specimen on a rusted gurney.

"You need to hide." He whispered. I stepped away from the lantern's light, and hid in a dark shadow. The man stopped halfway down the hall, a cloud of confusion on his face as he noticed my lantern, I started to panic. "Must be one of the recruits." he mumbled to himself and walked through an open door.

"That was far too close." he said as I walked up to the cell, standing only inches away from him. He looked down at me. "They would have loved a new test subject."

"Test subject?" I asked nervously.

"That creature behind you used to go by the name Arian Xavier."

"He did that to him?"

"Not just him. There are a group of men on this ship called the Steel Elements."

"How did they do it…?"

"First they used a neuromuscular blocker, which made it hard to move. They used a variety of drugs and other tactics to brainwash them, and made them forget they're human."

I was speechless and I could tell he knew it frightened me.

He was concerned. "Does Aruno know that you are down here?"

"Not at all…"

"I think maybe you should leave."

"I don't want to go yet." He smiled. Possibly because I brought him the company he needed; to feel more human. He must have been alone here for more than a decade. He smiled and spoke curiously. "What caused you to run off with sky pirates other than to find Mrs. Kahara?"

"Uhh…" I looked down at my feet. "The uh… Raqoian army fleet came after me."

He looked startled. "Why would they be after you?"

"I uh… told the king off during his speech." I stuttered "A-and then started somewhat of a riot." I smiled nervously.

Kazuhiko looked frightened "Why would you do that?"

"I didn't mean to. He well… He had it coming."

"That he did." He smiled once more. "During his speech, did he mention anything about my sister?"

"There's a Raqoian Princess?" I was puzzled, *I've never heard of her.*

For a brief moment I saw his left eye flash fluorescent, it glistened red for a moment then faded to normal. "Orfeo only wants power. He will never help our countries." He clenched his fist, in anger. "He doesn't deserve to be alive."

"Is the King that terrible?" I added sarcastically, "I thought he loved all people."

"You know very well he doesn't. He will never get away with this."

He seemed angry but I wasn't entirely sure. I stood still, "And what about the Raqoian Princess, Lady Kenzai?"

"Orfeo had her arrested," his voice rattled with anxiety, "Kenzai needed my help last time we spoke, and I... couldn't help her."

"Would it be alright if you told me?"

While smiling he said, "I could show you." He turned his head from me, putting his hand up to his fixed eye. A dim light gradually grew brighter shining through the interspaces between his fingers.

He lowered his hand, making a projection of moving pictures on the wall. Muffled sound seemed to follow the pyramid of light and echoed in the cell.

I stared at the mysterious light, astonished. *How could this be coming from his eye?* The pictures looked so vivid. The motion of them seemed to draw me closer.

"Kazuhiko, I've discovered the reason for Orfeo's parricide." A young lady came into view, with long auburn layered wavy hair. Her feet looked dusty from the dirty ground. She was wearing pale white hakama pants which had a variety of different designs in a deep black ink that made her waist seem very slim.

She was wearing a white shirt with long sleeves which came down to her elbow, and a black corset with metal gear outcroppings over top. She was standing in an elevated corner of a musty tavern. "I don't have much time to explain." She looked around frantically.

"Go ahead. We have enough time."

"I found out..." she hesitated "I'm meant to rule as appointed queen over Raqoia, until you marry a Vermyrian."

"But, its okay isn't it? Now we can take back the crown."

"No it isn't! He found out that I know. He's forcing me to sign documents which invalidate my queen-ship. Brother, you need to stop him!"

A woman ran, gliding up behind her. She was about five foot eight, and wore a dark purple, gold and maroon wave textile henna dress. Covering her face as she spoke was a dark multi colored scarf.

Her eyes were lined with dark paint. "Lady Kenzai, we have been compromised. The Nobel guards were right behind me." Her voice sounded faint and familiar to me.

Kazuhiko started to speak but the woman interrupted him "Kazuhiko, you can't let them know you are here.

They just want us. We'll make for your escape." She glanced around, and then stared him straight in his eyes, "You need to leave now!" This woman had to have been my mother! He told me that he knew her or rather, hasn't seen her in a long time.

He nodded to Kenzai "I'll see what I can do about Orfeo's documents." Before he left, Kenzai looked to her brother, her young face full of concern.

Luna was behind her, picking up a glass bottle from the bar as she strode by. Kazuhiko walked slowly down the stairs and towards the door beside the bar. The barkeep tried to stop him, waving his arms in front of him. During this, a loud disturbance erupted from the entrance. The bartender left the projector frame to calm the uproar.

Kazuhiko entered through the door and into a dark messy kitchen, pots and pans clustered about on tables and around the floor. He followed the light on the wall, and found a pass-through window to look out of. He crouched low and peered above him into the dining hall.

Kenzai had already left the scene, but Luna stayed back, in an effort to distract the guards. She flung off her dark Bedouin cover up, revealing full leather armor. The entrance doors flung open, as two Nobles in black metallic armor walked in.

She lifted a chair and threw it toward the door, it bashed against one of the guards, forcing him to stumble. The other ran at her, swinging a pole in her direction. She swung her leg, kicking it out of the man's hand. More guards swept into the tavern. The man continued to fight her, but she lifted an empty bottle latched onto the side of her belt, and threw it. The glass shattered across his helm and lodged out of various openings. He struggled to take his helmet off; the glass effectively blinded him, and tripped backward into the crowd of guards.

Suddenly a large block of fire wood clashed through the tavern's front stained glass windows. Three citizens were knocked in the head and sprawled out on the floor, struggling to pull themselves up.

More Nobles ran into the tavern, holding pole axes as they poured into the room, surrounding my mother. Luna lifted up a shield she found from a guard, who was laid out on a floor, unable to move.

The Nobles closed in on her, two of them slashed at her right and on her left. She held the shield up fending off the guards' attacks, hitting the Noble left of her in the jugular sending him backwards gagging.

In the same act, she shoved the right guard away with her shield then launched forward, and swing kicked the third, face planting him into the ground. The citizens ran toward the back doors, panicking as some other chaos erupted behind her.

She paid no attention to the crowd, she faced her opponents fiercely. They seemed a little more apprehensive about charging her.

One guard ran to grab a stool but the barkeep ripped it from his grasp and knocked them over the head with it.

Another guard followed suit, swinging a pole into the crowd. Another ran past Luna but she kicked him back into the throng, they trampled him, cracking his bones. Kazuhiko looked away from the fight for a moment.

As this happened a guard from behind lunged at her and kicked her on the ground. As she fell she held the shield up, protecting her body from the oncoming attack. She kicked outward at them in the stomach. Some faltered and fell away while others continued on with the attack.

The projection on the cracked cell blurred as Kazuhiko shifted to see her again. When he came to a stop the guards lifted Luna off of the ground and held her between them.

They had captured her but she wasn't finished yet. She turned sideways and using her upper body strength, flung the guard to her left as she kicked the one on her right in the torso.

She picked up the nearest chair and bashed a guard in the head, causing him to fall; he knocked out the one behind him like a game of dominos.

She was grabbed again from behind but this time three guards held her down. She struggled but to no avail. She screamed at them in anger as they lifted her up, holding her with her arms behind her back.

She stopped struggling when the room around her became eerily quiet. The citizens stopped jeering and the Nobles turned about to see why everyone became frightened. The Nobles held her tightly and she scowled at the entrance.

The sound of a few pairs of boots filled the now silent tavern. Orfeo calmly walked into frame, in full black and red shogun armor. His presence and size was very imposing, something I hadn't really noticed from when he gave his speech; but I hadn't been that close, and had never seen him in armor.

He stood in place beside Luna. She looked fearful, but Orfeo, paying no attention to her, looked straight ahead. From the left side came two more Noble guards in shinny black metallic armor, who must have came in through the spare entrance. They held a person between them.

They thrust Lady Kenzai to her knees in front of Orfeo.

"Why did you leave home for this peasant tavern?"

She paused and seemed perturbed by the question, but I gathered that Orfeo was not confident in personal conversations; such as it is with men who think they own the world.

"I snuck out to get away from the castle life, and Miss Kahara followed me. She was only trying to stop me."

"Is that why she attacked my guards?"

Kenzai spoke slowly, signs of irritation viable in her expression. "No, my king... we... came here to meet a leader of the resistance against you. But he never showed his face in our presence."

"That mangy rat has obviously swindled us!" Luna piped up, but then angrily cowered again, her hair falling in her face as she looked away from Orfeo; he set his silent gaze on her.

He smiled very obnoxiously, as if he knew they were lying. "Very well," now his gaze fixed coldly on Kenzai. "Lady Kenzai is a traitor to the people of Raqoia, Her King, and her empire."

Kenzai was on the verge of tears. Whether from anger or frustration, it was hard to tell which. Luna got up the courage to yell out, "Don't listen to him child, he is a coward!" The Noble to her left slapped her across the face. Orfeo raised his hand to calm his guards from proceeding further. He turned his back on them, facing all the citizens and soldiers standing within the tavern.

He spoke loudly to his men, in an orderly tone, "This village is a harbor for dissidents and criminals. Burn it to the ground. Send half the inhabitants to work camps and the other half to resettlement in the Native lands."

Kenzai was devastated, and Luna had rage boiling inside of her, and looked at Orfeo's back in disgust. The guards walked over to Kenzai, but before I could see what had happened, the image started to blur. Then the image faded away all together.

Kazuhiko in the cell was resetting his eye, and silently weeping with the other. He seemed visibly weakened by watching the projection. I wasn't really sure why he had even shown it to me; perhaps he plays the image over and over to himself. He wiped away his tears and regained his self composure. "I need to save her."

"If I could help you escape, would you help me? I need to leave the Annabeth. I'm not quite sure if I can handle living here."

His expression changed and he seemed intrigued by my question. "You wouldn't understand what helping me would entail." He grinned. "I'll help you, sure."

"Alright, deal." I smiled back at him.

"Zathena," I felt someone grab my shoulder. I swiftly looked behind me. Satomi stood shaking. "I thought something horrible happened to you."

"Almost."

Clanking and hissing noises came from behind Satomi. She turned around to find the creature standing behind the bars staring at us. She jumped in fright. "That thing is not human."

"Well, aren't you the smart one." Kazuhiko joked playfully. I laughed along.

"Who is this jerk?" She jumped when seeing his scarred face but continued to grimace at him.

"Uhh… Satomi, this is the prince of Raqoia. Kazuhiko Mirashikari."

"Aruno has told me so much about you, Satomi." he grinned.

"He has?" Satomi said confused and a tad bit disturbed.

"How did you learn all of this?" I said perplexed.

He smiled again. "What can I say, I am the Prince."

I opened up my satchel bag, pulling out the key shaped like a dragon.

"Zathena! What are you doing?"

"I need to help him escape."

"What? Why is he in there to begin with?"

Kazuhiko said irritated. "Aruno thinks I am going to die, fighting my brother."

"You're not actually going to try to kill him? Right?"

"He has an entire army backing him." He slightly raised his voice enough to show his anger. "Why in god's name would I try killing him without an equal force?"

I put the key in the lock, but Satomi stopped me again. "Satomi, I don't know what those men will do to him, and honestly, I don't want to find out." I pushed her away from me as I turned the key. Kazuhiko slowly opened the door, as I stepped backward.

He stood in front of me, and the genuine smile on his face made him seem more like a human, and less like a man made 'monster'. A moment passed and I caught myself smiling back at him.

Kazuhiko caressed my cheek and tilted my head. He leaned closer to me and kissed me on the forehead. "Thanks love." He whispered then, he took off running opposite of the stairs.

Satomi asked. "Where is he going?"

I said absent mindedly, "I don't know…" I giggled awkwardly afterward.

"I don't get it… the exit is that way...?" Satomi pointed toward the stairs.

"Satomi? The prince kissed me."

Satomi waved her hand in front of my face, "Snap out of it!" She demanded.

I shut the cell door locking it. "Uh, Satomi?" I stared at the locked door.

"What?" She asked confused.

"You know, I just remembered something."

Satomi stood startled. "And that is?" She already knew the answer.

"We forgot to lock Aruno's door back."

I turned around to leave; the creature of a man was still watching us. His dark wide eyes followed our motions. We walked away to the stairs and slowly ascended them to the main platform.

Behind the white door I could hear the mechanical industrial noises all too familiar now. I opened the door, and looked around, everything seemed like it was fine.

Satomi ran in front of me, pushing me aside. She turned the corner but stopped suddenly staggering backward in shock. I whispered. "What is it?"

She came back and pressed against the wall, and urged me to as well. She bent down and we peered around the corner, and I looked right above her. Aruno and Melvin were walking down the long corridor.

Aruno carried a gun.

"What are we going to do?"

"Zathena!" Aruno turned the corner. His face was contorted with rage and the grip around his pistol's old and worn mahogany handle seemed to be tightening.

The brassy, scratched metal glinted dimly yet dismay-ingly. Satomi stepped backward. "Aruno." She said in shock.

"Did you both honestly think you could steal from me, and get away with it?"

Satomi pointed her finger at me. "It was her idea, I swear."

"Satomi!" I cried.

Aruno's gun was pointed straight at me then. Time started to slow down within my mind. My heart raced but I stood still. The blood racing through my veins now chilled like ice. I could feel adrenaline shake through me, rattling my nerves. Melvin looked frightened at the sight of Aruno's anger. "Do not move." Aruno demanded.

CHAPTER 9
Steel Elements

*T*here was a red flash of hot smoke as he pulled the trigger. The sound of the gunshot blasted through my ear drums and echoed through the back of my mind. There was the distinct sound of a bullet tearing through flesh. I fell to the ground, utterly shocked. My body was shaking, I felt cold, and began to feel for a wound.

I opened my eyes looking upward.

"How would I shoot you?" Aruno said, standing above me, smiling. He gave me his hand while calling in on a brass voice transmitter in his right. "Steel Elements be on the lookout; we've had a prisoner escape." He pulled me up slowly, my knees shaking, I felt scared and disoriented. I looked behind me, and jumped at the sight.

On the ground was a gaunt gray thing, with his jaw blasted off, and blood pooling around him seeping out of the area where his mouth once was. I backed away gasping in horror. Satomi screamed and ran behind Aruno.

Rubbing his head, he asked exasperated. "Did you let it out?"

"No," I cried, "I didn't even go near him…!"

Melvin walked towards the body. "There's no way that thing could have gotten out on its own, Captain."

"Looks like it's pork chops tonight, Melvin." Aruno joked.

Melvin grimaced and nudged it with his foot. For a big guy, he seemed pretty squeamish, and winced at the thing as if it were a roach. "Ye should call in for a cleanup, cap't."

"We'll take care of it after we make sure the prison's secure. Zathena, hand them over." Aruno demanded.

"Hand what over?"

"The keys." he stated effortlessly. I dug in my satchel bag for the keys, but only found two.

I handed them over. "Well, I will be going now…" I attempted to walk away.

"And why do you think that?" Aruno raised his eyebrow, "How about we go meet the Steel Elements?"

"I'm not going down there again! And I don't want to meet the Steel Elements." I said frightened.

Melvin muttered to himself, "So now you don't want to go down there hmm?"

"I don't say I blame her…" Satomi agreed.

"After this stunt you don't really have a choice in the matter."

"But…" I was stunned by my fear, "I'm not going?"

"Yea you are, let's go." He grabbed Satomi and me by our arms, dragging us through the door. We walked over the dead experiment on the floor, completely steering clear of him. Melvin didn't walk with us, but cowardly shut the door for us.

"Let go of us!" I shouted. He released his grip angered, but soon cooled.

"Why would you think it was okay to come down here?" Aggravation withheld in his voice.

"I wanted to know what you were hiding." I could only show resentment in my words. I was filled with indignation. I reassured myself. Satomi stood by the railing in silence.

"And what did you find out?"

"I found out about the creatures, and that maybe I should have followed your rules," I felt my throat tightening. "I just want to find my mother." He stood staring at me, his look expressionless.

"I don't have time for this." He muttered and continued to walk down the stairs. He held no emotion, and I was on the brink of tears. Why am I even here? Satomi followed Aruno, and so did I. I knew I had to follow him, I had no other choice.

Are they going to keep me and Satomi down here for some sick experiment? How could he want to hurt people like this, it was the most cringing thing I could think of.

I steered away from thoughts about the creature dying behind me, and only focused in front of me. The thought hit me; *what exactly did Aruno mean by 'How about we go meet the Steel Elements?'* I glanced behind me, Satomi looked like she really wanted to say something snarky, and Aruno looked quite irritated.

A call sounded over Aruno's radio and he quickened his pace "All hands: Full ship lockdown. Seal all non-essential passages and await further protocol."

The light was brighter downstairs, and as I came to the bottom, a group of five men walked toward us.

One wore a dirty white bandana cap with a hazard menacing sign lightly dyed red. He had on a dirty light brown medical mask with the same symbol, indicating something or another.

Maybe the symbol stood for them being part of the Steel Elements, but I wasn't sure what exactly the Steel Elements were; maybe a mercenary group.

It was hard to concentrate on his eyes, because he wore a fogged lens spotlight in his metal shoulder plate; but I thought his eyes were a bit gray. His black laboratory coat was tied up with large yellow buttons and a narrow red lab apron. His brown tool belt held medical instruments.

The man next to him was unnaturally large with the same menacing radiation sign over a black pressure suit and brigandine. He wore a double thigh holster and a small receiver hooked on a three pistol baldric. His face was covered by a dense gas mask. This one kind of reminded me of a sadistic knight.

Beside him, a tall skinny man who had a face covered by a mirror mask. He had corked vials on a baldric over a long black and yellow hooded doublet. And the sign from the other two rested on his metal shoulder plate. He wore long gloves up past his elbow and black boots with white coverings.

The man alongside him gave me cold chills. He had an electronic pack hooked to his left arm, and wires looped around a steel bolted gorget to the fingers of this right hand, which from his gloves bright static bolts dance. He wore a light brown laboratory coat, with black steel toe boots. Welding goggles over his eyes, reflecting red in the light. He too had the same symbol as the others.

Finally, the man who appeared to be leading them all was the same one who I saw earlier with the rusted gurney. He was bald, but with a goatee. Black welding glasses hid his eyes. They halted in front of Aruno staring menacingly. I took a step backward. They looked frightening.

"Are the prisoners accounted for?"

"We were just about to come find you," The leader's voice was deep and grungy with an accent like Sir Jonny, but more elegant. "Prisoner in cell twenty-nine escaped."

Aruno looked at me, anger arose in his voice. "I'm guessing you had nothing to do with this?"

I looked forward at the group of men and then back to Aruno shaking my head.

"Satomi," he looked at her intently. "did she?"

She glanced down. "Nope." He walked past me, toward her. I could see him whisper something in her ear, her face flushed white with a look of shock. She shook her head and proceeded to whisper something back to him. He looked at her and then glanced over at me. I avoided all eye contact with him, and stared ahead. The leader stood with his arms behind his back. His eyes were obscured behind his goggles; each member had some part of their face hidden along with their eyes. His lips produced a crooked, wicked grin.

"Zathena." Aruno stood beside me, his voice booming. "Are you positive you don't know where he went?"

"No, I… don't."

He rested his hand on my back. "Would you men mind keeping her until she tells us?"

"N-n-no!" I moved over, pushing him away. I cried, "Okay, I'll tell you everything!" I explained surely. "I met Kazuhiko and then I did, I let him out- but then he ran that way!" I spoke with ire which convinced Aruno and his group. "I really don't know where he is now, honestly."

"I had a feeling you would do that if you met him. The helpless prince locked away; what little girl could resist?" Aruno spoke solemnly and ironically, almost to himself. "I take you away from almost certain death, give you a *nice* place to live, and you break every rule on the very first day you're here."

My voice cracked with rage and hot tears streamed across my face from the sunken fear in my gut.

"You didn't give me any reason to trust you! You lied to me about the most important thing in the world."

"You don't need to trust me - probably shouldn't, given the kind of man I am." he sneered at the saying, than spoke bluntly, and without sign of hostility. "Yet, you don't have a choice."

I clenched the heavy top layer of my skirt, and looked down at the floor. My messy hair hung in the space around drops of falling tears. I was entirely choleric.

The leader broke the silence "If you're done with this drama, we have another to attend to. Please meet me in the conference room." He turned back toward me. "Go to your room," He glanced over to Satomi. "Both of you."

Aruno agreed. "Go on then."

I turned around to leave wiping the tears from my eyes. Following Satomi, I walked steadily but hurriedly up the stairs. As we walked into the boiler room, shutting the door behind us, Satomi still said nothing. She looked on the brink of tears herself.

The fact that she blamed everything on me was a little annoying for the fact that she went along with it and accepted doing it.

Then suddenly she spoke, "I'm sorry I made you feel like I betrayed you…"

"It wasn't all my idea, you wanted to come also - but I'm not even worried about that. I understand why you blamed me, and it does not bother me." We stopped talking for a couple of minutes. "But, Satomi," She looked over at me.

"Why were you so quick to tell him? What did he say to you?"

We were standing in the middle of the boiler room; the men shoveling coal did not seem to mind our presence once more. It made me wonder as to what they were thinking about us. She looked behind her and continued to walk a couple of yards, stopping a good three feet away from the entry.

"He told me that, if you told him the truth, you wouldn't end up like the man that gave you the idea to break the rules in the first place."

"Avner? What happened to him?"

"The Steel Elements took him, put him in a cell." she sounded scared by her own words, "I'm sorry, I told Aruno I wouldn't be able to live with myself if I knew something like that happened to you."

"It's okay." Satomi walked ahead of me, leaving the area. Now some of the men stopped working, staring my way annoyed. One swung his sledgehammer over his shoulder, blackened by the coal dust and droplets of sweat leaving streaks down his body. Another man walked toward me slowly, shooing me off.

Feeling uncomfortable I backed away, leaving the boiler room. Satomi was a few steps ahead of me when I ran up to her. After finding out the entire reason to why I came here was a lie, I really saw no reason to why I had to live here anymore. I always jumped around to different homes when I was little. *Just another mistake.*

I spotted Zilpher from across the room. He looked invigorated and not in any way exhausted from training. His light brown shaggy hair and clothes weren't mangled in anyway.

Zilpher looked over and walked our way, "What happened? Did you find out anything?" He questioned smiling.

"Aruno found out that we broke into his room."

"I know as much, he said something to Jonny about it."

"What did he tell him?"

"He asked Jonny if he knew when you both come through here. What did you find out?"

Satomi explained the entire situation, without mentioning Kazuhiko. "Aruno's really angry; I thought the Steel Elements were going to kill us."

Zilpher seemed confused, "The what?"

"The Steel Elements. They're a group of men, that conduct human experiments or something behind the white door," I quickly informed him. "To be honest, I was only curious, I really thought maybe someone knew where my mother was, and he did. I'm seriously done, there's no reason to be here anymore."

Satomi stated argumentatively, "How is being here, worse than being on the streets of Versalen?"

"There are no rules out there on my own; I lived by my own rules."

"Zathena," Zilpher started. "There's always a reason for where you end up." I ignored his statement.

We all walked downstairs and Zilpher left the lobby first.

"Hey, Zathena, at least we get the whole day off!" Satomi was smiling ear-to-ear

"Yeah? To slouch in our rooms and do absolutely nothing."

"He only made us go to our rooms so we wouldn't get in the way."

I snapped. "What is wrong with you? Why are you so naive?"

"What?" Her eyes were glistening and started to water.

"Satomi, I'm sorry I just-" A group of men turned the corner, but we avoided them by walking behind a bookshelf. I reproached in a whispered tone, "I don't understand why you trust Aruno. Ever since you saw him you've been on his side!"

She looked down. "It's not about him. It has never been about him." She looked up, "It's only ever been about sky pirates, the adventure! Feeling the wind on my face and through my hair when I walk on deck! I want to be remembered; being part of a crew that actually cares about something. I want to be someone; I would rather die being a sky pirate, then a low life peasant!"

"That's just a dream," I said laughing. "What skills could make you a sky pirate!" I smiled as I hugged her. "Satomi, you're on an airship, you're technically a sky pirate already!"

As I let go of her she smiled at me. "I'm going to head off."

"I will later," I smiled. "There's this book I need to find. I forgot to take it with me last night.

"Alright." She nodded at me then turned around heading to her room. I pushed some books aside on the shelf, watching Satomi as she left. As she turned the corner a man in a gasmask ran into her. She about fell over when he caught her. "Are you okay?" His voice muffled.

She laughed, "Oh yes, I am fine." Soon after, he nodded his head and walked away.

The lobby gave me such a strange feeling. There was something about it I couldn't quite understand. It was sort of just a library with boards holding the books in the shelves, an eerie glow cast through them from the moonlight leading through the windows. In the middle of the room, a glass flying fish statue held many varieties of ferns in its stomach. Its vast crystal wings covering about two meters. Half of the lobby had darkened by lack of windows.

Intense activity from the other half; pirates ran about and checked up on things. I walked toward the furthest back shelve; dimmed lights cast strange shadows which reminded me of a dark seedy tavern. I looked through the books, than a quick movement beside me caught my attention.

"This is a really nice book," Kazuhiko mentioned, sitting in the darkest of the sections. "I think you should read it." He got up tossing the book to me.

"Kazuhiko?" He stood close in front of me. "The entire ship is on lockdown, they are all looking for you."

"I know." He whispered, "I'm leaving tomorrow to locate my sister, and this is when I ask for your help."

"What do you want me to do?"

"Come with me, I don't want to leave you here alone."

"I won't be alone."

He held my hand. "Please you need to help me."

"I need to know that I can trust you." A frantic scene happened in the middle of the lobby, men began running about yelling at each other.

"I don't have much time. Meet me here tomorrow - if I'm not caught –" He looked around, "I will tell you everything you want to know." He smiled at me. "Goodnight." With the last words being said, he ran off.

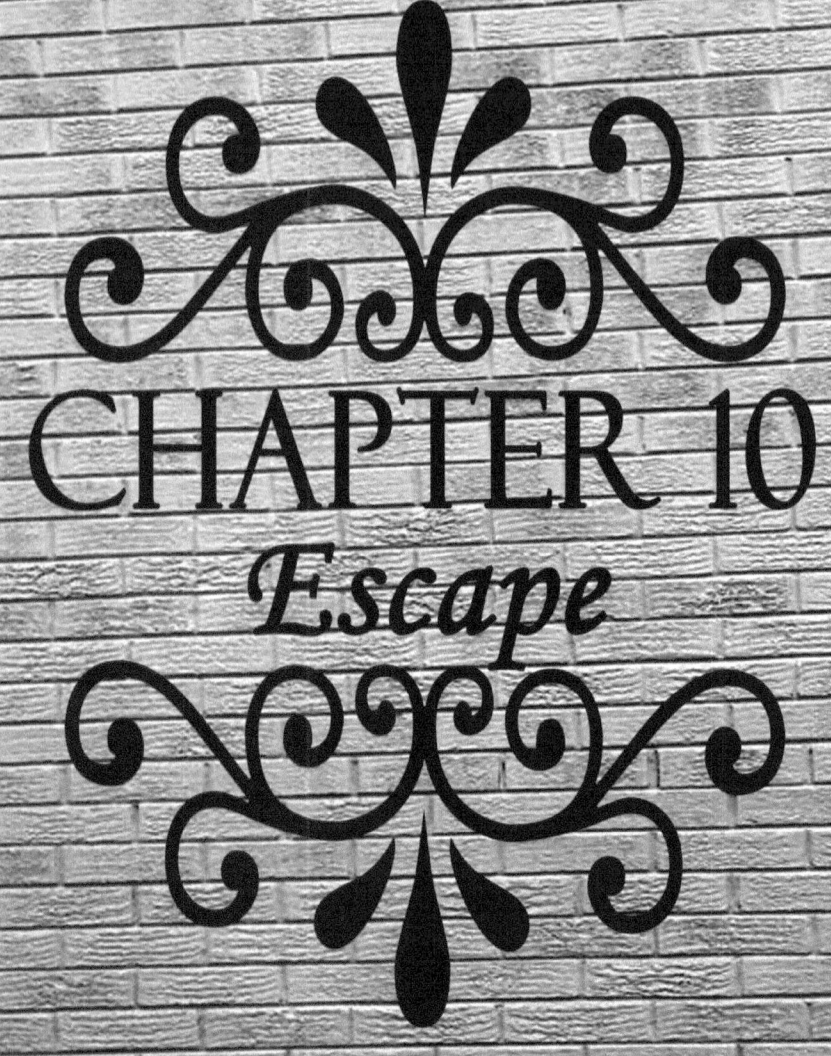

CHAPTER 10

Escape

I awoke to the sound of my own labored breath, lying on a cold concrete floor and as I tilted my head, looking up, I could not make out my surroundings. The room around me was darker than night and I could hear a familiar faint voice speaking in the distance, although I couldn't place my thoughts around who it was.

Now a dim light illuminated from in front of me, its rays growing intense as I pulled myself off of the floor. I stood in a room encased by metal bars. The ceiling was low, and I could hardly breathe from the anxiety that boiled inside.

I could feel my body shaking, adrenaline pumped through my veins. The stomach pains from hunger lingered and I felt dizzy. I walked toward the bars, trying to locate a door, but there was none.

I placed my hand on the iron, and it fell through. I couldn't grasp my mind around the situation; how this could be happening. I pushed my whole body through the solid bars.

"She's escaped!"

I swiftly spun around to my left. Men with the same symbol as the Steel Elements had seen me falling through the cell. I took off running to the right, straight to the winding staircase. They ran after me, and the hallway seemed to have no end. I could feel my heart rate go up, and my breathing became a hassle. Then standing at the bottom of the stairs waiting for me, was Aruno. As I ran inches past him, he grabbed my arm stopping me.

As I looked behind me at him, the people chasing me, I tried to pull away. His being began violently changing; morphing into the ugly gray thing Kazuhiko had called Erian Xavier. His skin on my arm felt grating, and rough; his long nails I could feel piercing through my arm. I screamed in horror then immediately fell through the floor.

I landed in the library, knocking all the air from my lungs. I could hear the same loud growling. I looked behind me, thinking they had followed me.

While thinking of it, they then appeared behind me. I lifted off the floor and far off in front of me, Kazuhiko stood with his back to me. I glanced over my shoulder frightened when I noticed the leader of the Steel Elements walking towards me. I quickened my pace towards the prince.

"Kazuhiko?"

To get his attention, I reached for him, but just as I did he turned around. It was never Kazuhiko, but Orfeo. "Help me find my sister." His voice was echoed in symphony with Kazuhiko's. A static array jolted as his body shifted between the two as they spoke. I then felt a hand on my shoulder and an intense fright.

I opened my eyes, lying in my bed. Of course it was all merely a dream. Something soft was left in my arms, brown in color with fluff. I sat up, holding it outward to view it clearer. It was a teddy bear with a red bow tie. His right eye was held loosely by a yellow string and; I remembered this.

When I was young, my mother used to read me those stories of the great adventurer, the one they called Aruno. Then a year after the stories ended, my father bought me a teddy bear. I soon named that bear after the man my mother fancied, Aruno the Infamous. I loved those stories, and always thought about them, it led me to leave with him.

She took this toy with her when she left me. *No, who left this here? How is it here?* Frightened, and more enraged than anything, I threw the stuffed toy at the wall.

The creepy dream from last night, it felt so real, like I was there. Was it meant to mean anything? The thought about the dream overwhelmed me that morning and when I stood up to leave, I was already dressed from the night before.

I wore tight brown pants with black laced up boots and a thick long white sweater with my hair in a ponytail. I looked behind me before I left, Satomi was asleep still, and I thought she looked peaceful.

When I shut the door, I felt like someone was watching me, like my imaginations were taking form outside of my dreams. Something from the darkness was about to jump out. Something, I wanted nothing to do with.

I quickly walked to Zilpher's room hoping to catch him while he was awake. I quietly knocked on the door.

"Zilpher?" I heard him walk to the door, which he opened with a confused expression.

"Hi, can I come in?" I asked shyly.

"Of course," He moved away from the door, letting me walk through. "Is something the matter?"

"I can't be here anymore." I was standing in the middle of his room, thinking then about Kazuhiko, and what life he must have lived here. I stood there, silent for a moment, swept in my dreams still.

The room really was significantly decorated royally and it was meant to be for him. Zilpher stood next to me with a look of greater confusion. I continued and rambled on about the uneasy dream. "I had a vivid nightmare last night... I was downstairs and Aruno turned into one of those things and the Steel Elements were chasing me, but then I ended up in the lobby and found Kazuhiko, but when he turned around he was actually Orfeo."

"Slowdown, wait, who? Is there something about yesterday you haven't told me?"

I remembered how Satomi filled in for me, telling him about the room, and what laid down there, but she never told him the entire story. "Yes, Aruno wasn't only angry about us going down there; it may be also because I found who he locked away." Zilpher seemed even more confused now than he had been. "Aruno lied to us when he said the prince no longer lived here. I found him yesterday."

"What did you do?" He looked a bit worried.

"He was so alone and depressed, I just had to let him escape," I abruptly said, too quickly to filter my thoughts. "You should have seen what they did to him!" I paused, realizing I had spoken too loudly. If I told Zilpher about the prince's eye and what the Steel Elements did to him, I knew it would only confuse him further, so I improvised. "The entire left side of his face was mutilated."

"Are you positive he was the prince?" His question completely caught me off guard. I saw the prince's face; I recalled that they matched the pictures I had seen when I was in Versalen.

"What? Yes I'm sure. We all saw the plaque outside your room."

I began to feel that he was in fact right, but I knew for certain that it was him. I thought more about his face, the scars and the pain he must have felt.

How his eye was intriguingly mechanical in design and how he had kissed me. There was no second guessing it: It had to be him.

Zilpher seemed to reconsider his last question. "I guess it would make sense." He looked up, around the room and then back at me. "Do you know where he is now?"

"I uhh..." I thought about telling him that very second, but I knew I shouldn't. I knew he wouldn't understand. How could I tell him that I was planning on leaving with the prince? "No, he ran off last I saw him."

He slightly tilted his head. "Are you lying to me?"

I began to feel uneasy. "No! How could I lie to you?"

"Alright, I was only wondering."

I looked down, thinking of a possible way to sidetrack him from my horrible essence of lying. "It's okay," I turned my head away from him. "Aruno didn't believe me when I told him either. He dragged me down there yesterday and tried to scare me by saying he'd lock me away if I lied. I saw the Steel Elements and I have seen what they do to people… To people like me."

I looked back at him dejected. "I'm afraid for my life because I let the prince escape. I don't know what's going to happen to me. I don't know what he's going to do." At that moment, I did not care to cry in front of him; he was my only brother and I loved him.

My arms stayed near my sides, as he wrapped me in his arms, holding me close. "I won't let them hurt you." He let go of me, stepping backward. "Please stop crying." He wiped away my tears, smiling. I looked down at my feet, trying to conceal my tense smile. "I'm going to find a way to get us out of here, just the two of us. We can leave tomorrow, together."

I gazed up at him. "What if they find out?"

He smiled, "Don't worry; I'll keep you safe."

I asked skeptically, "There are two hundred people on this airship and they all follow Aruno's commands, and you're only one person."

He laughed lightly, "I could get us out of here, *before* that becomes a problem."

I didn't understand what he was trying to tell me. If I were to leave with him tomorrow, and someone did find out, how would he be able to get us out without someone noticing? I was to leave that morning, but I didn't want to leave without my brother. *What if I don't come back tomorrow? Zilpher will be left here with Satomi, and would probably think that I would be dead.*

"But, what if I'm not here tomorrow?" I questioned.

"Why would that happen?" The creases in his face showed clear signs of misunderstanding. I wanted to tell him then, but surely he wouldn't understand.

"I don't know."

He became irritated, "Zathena, what are you not telling me?" I felt like I should have given up the conversation and ran away that very second. I hated how I was so horrible at lying. This made me think. *How did I survive all those years stealing from people?*

"Uhh," I looked away from him, my horrible lies showing. I decided to evade the question by asking another. "Nothing really, but what if my dream was trying to tell me something? What if they come back for me?"

"Everyone is too busy looking for the prince; his ransom is high; besides I wouldn't let them take you." I smiled at the thought of having a brother who is willing to spare his life for me, but the thought of the prince being sold for ransom disgusted me.

"I'm okay now; I think I'll just stay in my room." I didn't want the prince leaving without me, and I felt like that was going to happen.

"I think that might be best. Be careful if you find the prince again, who knows what his motives are."

I walked out of Zilpher's room annoyed, and back into my room to pick up the book from last night off the Pugin table.

He doesn't even know the prince; I doubt he's anything like his brother. How could he be?

I heard more people running down the corridor, yelling about something. I looked at Satomi again, thinking she must have woken up from those loud drunkards.

She was moving frantically, kicking the blankets off of her. "Satomi!" I cried, but still, she didn't wake up. I walked over to her, knowing she was having a nightmare. I pushed her shoulder and she woke up yelling. "Satomi! Are you okay?" Seeing her freaking out reminded me of how I felt when I woke up.

She looked at me aghast. "Zathena? I had a dream that you were thrown overboard!"

"I would never die that way," I laughed. "I had a nightmare last night as well."

"Did I die?"

"No, I could never picture you dying, I love you too much." I laughed, which made her smile. I felt like I made her feel better, she no longer looked concerned. "I'm going back to the library; I really enjoyed being there last night."

"Is it because of the prince?"

I said sarcastically, "No, I just like looking out of the windows, and seeing the many faces." I rolled my eyes.

"Okay, I'll come later, but seriously, stay out of trouble."

"What do you take me for? A bootlegger?" I left the room laughing, and walked down the hardwood floor to the library. *I wonder why she and I both had nightmares.* I quickened my pace in the silence of the halls, anxious to meet with Kazuhiko.

At the end of the hall, standing in the open door, was the man who gave me the key to Aruno's room.

"Avner?"

He was leaning against the archway with his feet partially in the hall and in the library, as if he were waiting for me. As I approached he turned his head at me and squinted as if trying to recall something. As I got within a few feet of him, his confounded look instantly faded.

"Well, what's a pretty lady like *you* doing on this airship?" he asked provocatively.

"Avner, you don't remember me?" I asked.

"I think I would remember a beautiful lady like you?" he reached out to take my hand but I pulled it away.

Something horrible must have happened. Something was wrong with him. "Two days ago you gave me the key to Aruno's room. I heard they took you aw-"

I stopped as he jerked his hand away and began furiously scraping it with his nails.

"Avner, are you okay?"

He was now chewing on his fingers and began speaking faintly, almost to himself. "Look, uh…" He immediately stopped his feral behavior and stared ahead blankly as he spoke "I have to go… clean up." he pulled away quickly and started to leave down the hall behind me, but tripped. I ran to help him up, but the grown man recoiled and shivered. He looked at me in the eyes, still for a second, than shrieked loudly "No! Get away!" he sat up using his hands, rolled over, got onto his feet, sprinting off to the command deck.

Okay, that's it. I need to get out of here. I thought to myself.

As I quickened my pace to the back corner behind the shelves, I looked through the massive teardrop windows above; the morning sky was a stormy dark blue, but seemed just as calm and still as the vast library around me.

Light flashed, brightening the dark room, mounted lights flickered. I looked back out the window seeing a fading trail of lightning, reaching from the clouds below.

I searched the dark nook sitting area for signs of the prince, but he was not there yet. I sat down in a chair, and thought, *maybe he decided to leave without me?*

I thought about reading the book Kazuhiko wanted me to read, the one Jonny had given me. The dust-stained gray leather cover was worn and title-less. I felt the soft square indented design of the cover. It seemed a very well crafted, expensive item; my parents never bought me something so exquisite. The prologue read simply "To Darling Gracilyn". Its first page was a black and white, block print photo of an exotic villa with an extravagant garden, and the caption on the page beside it was a poem.

The green, yellow and rainbow hair
That our earth doth bear,
A simply beauty without care
In that garden there

Pardon the envelope of color
The swath of niceties that our mother
Earth will show to the eyes of another

I continued flipping through pages, filled with dreamy stories, prints of cities in clouds, and more poems. About a third of the way through was a print of the castle Versalen.

As I examined it, Kazuhiko emerged from a dark corridor, his clothes covered in soot. He was carrying a burlap messenger bag, probably filled with food of some sort. "You're here? I got us some provisions for the trip last night. Wasn't easy sneaking into the kitchen with the cooks, and the crew members stalking about."

"Where are we going?" I sat up straight and closed the book; stared at him wondering.

"There's a village nearby, an old friend of mine lives there, he can help us find Lady Kenzai. I managed to get a reading of our latitude and longitude while on the bridge-"

I interrupted. "Uh, I want to go with you, but what about my friends? I mean I want to go, but I can't just leave without saying goodbye."

"I promise we'll come back for them once we've rescued Lady Kenzai. I will explain more on the way to the city. But right now we have to get going." He started to walk away, but stopped realizing I wasn't following him. "Are you coming?" He smirked, "I'll be bored without you."

"Okay. I'll come with you." The anxiety was familiar to me. I had the same panicked feelings from when I was met with the Noble guards who took me away when I was younger, the same feelings I had when I left a place meant to be my home.

I stood up to follow Kazuhiko as he walked around the bookcases.

"How did you stay hidden with the whole ship looking for you last night?"

"By staying quiet." He whispered and grinned smugly.

We stayed silent for a moment and could hear the ships engine thudding and pipes hissing. Faint thunder broke out around the ship as the sky flashed bright causing the lights to again flicker amongst the dark room.

"This doesn't feel right. Where is everyone?"

"Avner took off down the hall, which was strange... I figure the rest are possibly having a briefing over my escape. I'm really not quite sure."

"I heard people frantically running before I left my room, maybe something else is happening?"

"No...no..." He shook his head. "They know that if Aruno calls in for a briefing they can't keep him waiting."

"I guess I never really thought about his authority over the entire ship. I only read about the jobs he completed alone." Kazuhiko grabbed my hand.

He smiled at me, and almost laughed. "You know, you're very naïve. Aruno has vast authority, more then you understand. I'm surprised you are not afraid to be leaving with me. You have great courage, and I'm glad that I've met you." With that he hugged me. "Now, we must be careful."

We walked up the two tiered floors on our way to the stern deck. A brisk gust of wind swept into the library as he opened the doors, turning pages of books on podiums and filling my nose with the smell of rain. As soon as I got up onto the deck platform, he closed the doors behind me.

"Alright, the stairwell at the end of the stern leads to the gyrocycle hangar. When we open the loft doors, we should be quickly noticed; don't slow us down. Stay unnoticed, act normal."

We sprinted across the partially wet deck together, and found the triangular deck top stairwell to the hangar. He calmly reached into his bag and quickly retrieved what I recognized as a bump key.

He plunged it into the hangar door's simple lock and quickly turned. We went down the cramped and dark stairwell together; the walls were like the rich timbers of the ship's external hull. The hangar itself had a metal grate floor with about twenty-five gyrocycles covered in brown tarps.

The right side of the room contained at least fifty plateau pyramid shaped metal boxes, each one about six feet long and four feet high. He seemed really interested in these and a bit confused. "This is concerning." He walked closer and studied them concerned. He mumbled to himself. "How could he have obtained this technology?"

"Kazuhiko, let's just get out of here!" I whispered irately.

He walked closer to me, and as if agreeing with me, he smiled, "More courageous then I thought, speaking informal to a prince." He went to the back of the hanger and pulled away a tarp, revealing a large, gleaming black steel bi-rotor, wide chassis gyrocycle.

It had a dusty burgundy stained leather seat which could easily seat two, embroidered in gold Raqoian text. Two shaft rotors were attached to mechanisms on the sides and a small stability rotor off the back of the vessel. All connected to a compact steam engine system, flanked by strong chrome ventilation pipes.

It was like Aruno's gyrocycle, but this one had large turbines replacing the sidecar seats. He opened a compartment behind the seat and inserted his bag, rummaging for a bit before pulling out a golden key with attached baubles.

That was when I realized, we were not stealing this gyrocycle, for it belonged to him. I felt confused and betrayed. Zilpher was right; what kind of motives could he have?

"I thought you were held captive? But you're one of them? This is yours?"

He laughed a little, smiling almost as if he felt nervous. Then; he tried changing the subject. Nervously smiling once more, he slowly put the key away in his back pocket. "What did Aruno say when he found out you snuck downstairs?"

"Don't ignore me!" Stunned, he looked away from me. I felt bad that I yelled at him. He was the only one willing to give me answers, and I felt like I hurt him. He then looked back toward me when I continued on with dreariness. "He was indignant when he found you missing."

"I'm sorry, he gets like that sometimes."

"Why are you saying sorry for him?"

He looked down, sighed slightly, laughing, "I'm not one of them." He paused, as if thinking for a moment. "Aruno is my uncle."

"Your uncle?" I was completely shocked. "He's a true Raqoian?" Out of all the things I questioned, this had to have been the most staggering. Aruno didn't seem to have had a Raqoian accent. My mother's stories never mentioned him being Raqoian. "He's royal? What?" I was so confused. *Why would he need to steal if he's loaded?*

"I know this sounds very overwhelming to you."

A slight metal rattling sound came from upstairs. "Dumb…door!" Someone had fumbled with the locks.

Kazuhiko whispered, "Come with me, or get caught." I remembered not answering him, and just standing there. "You need to make a decision." He looked apoplectic and pulled a lever on the wall closest to him. The mechanisms around the loft doors came to life, winding heavy gears, and the loft doors crept open clacking cogs.

A red light mounted on the wall began flashing, and a siren blared from the forward superstructure. Kazuhiko waded into the vehicle's sunken cockpit, settling with a yoke control at his waist, and gestured for me to get on behind him by nod of his head. "We have to leave now!"

I got on the back of his gyrocycle, and wrapped my arms around his torso, holding on loosely.

He turned the golden key and started the gyrocycle's ignition, the baubles on his key ring jangling as the engine roared to life, belting exhaust. Turbulent wind shortly followed; streams of gray-blue light shone into the dusty hangar.

The propellers kicked on and began rapidly spinning, sending dust particles rushing about the room, tarps flapped up from adjacent gyrocycles and my hair whipped in my face. Suddenly we repulsed from the floor with a jerk, as the cycle had been magnetized to the deck. I gripped tightly around his waist as the gyrocycle lifted out of the open hatch and hovered above the deck.

Men were running out the lobby doors, and toward the hangar, as Jonny shouted to them over a strong gust which messed his hair, and his coat pulled in the wind. He looked directly at me, clearly disappointed.

Kazuhiko pulled forward, racing across the remaining distance and swooped over the stern of the ship, angled downwards and started to descend. I felt nauseous as if the free-fall effect from the plummet pulled at every organ separately.

We must have been seven thousand feet in the air, above a large open, rolling field, and a winding system of shallow riverbeds. I tried my hardest to forget about the sinking feeling that loomed over me.

He was headed toward the tree line of an Abutyus forest. He adjusted the direction of the ships descent, trying to make it so we would land as we reached the trees.

We continued towards the forest keeping clear of populated areas. We reached the edge of the forest and continued to fly nearly over the tree line.

The forest shuttered as it braced against a downburst which sent bamboo flying in the wind and outer trees bending almost halfway to the ground.

We were now well away from the ship when I looked behind us and saw two strange gyrocycles shoot out of

Annabeth's hangar, each one arced out at about one-hundred-fifty degrees, headed in two directions, at tremendous speed in a V formation.

They were black, long and gaunt for gyrocycles and had rotors close in to the body of the ship for better maneuverability. A searchlight was shining from their craft base as if scraping the sky like lightening.

They turned and then rotated upside down and then pointed downwards nearly in unison. They used the maneuver to gain momentum and pulled up just over ground level at an insane speed, then sped after us covering ground faster then we could.

I spoke loudly near Kazuhiko's ear into the wind. "They're catching up!" But the air's harsh whistle was too loud, because not a word out of my mouth could be heard.

He looked back and caught sight of the speeding bikes, seeming to examine them for a second, their acceleration and constant movement.

He turned around, throwing a switch which reversed the rotors, sending us straight down about twice as fast. My stomach lurched. The now loudly screeching bikes circled overhead like vultures as they descended and wrapped around in a pipe motion.

The two riders were decked in leather, and seemed to be part of Aruno's main crew rather than the specialized Steel Elements.

One, who I identified as the young man whom I had met when we first arrived on the ship, accelerated ahead of us to the ground while the other prepared a miniature harpoon weapon.

He fired it and it sailed stiffly through the air, slightly ahead of us, and pierced through our cycle's metal haul. The projectile was attached to the gun by a chain. The pursuer linked the chain to the hover vehicle and yanked back.

Kazuhiko turned his attention to the clank of the harpoon striking his gyrocycle, pointed it out to me, mouthing "Take care of it!" I gripped him tighter and kicked at it hoping to dislodge it, but it was hooked quite firmly in the cycle's hull. I mouthed back to Kazuhiko "It won't move!"

We were nearing the tree level now, and the cycle rider ahead of us had slowed and turned broadside in our path.

The cycle chained to us had turned its bottom end at us and our gyrocycle shook as the pilot tried to slow us down by vectoring his cycle's power the opposite direction.

I knew we were going to be brought down soon. So I decided to have another go at dislodging the harpoon. I held onto the gyrocycle and tried reaching the hook piercing our side, but my hand was about a foot too short.

I pushed Kazuhiko's shoulder hard, frightened. He looked back quickly, pointing at the boot and I could faintly hear him yell, "Use something to get it out!"

He seemed to have maintained focus on what to do if the two riders' plan succeeded. I turned around in my seat, and opened the storage behind me. A strong cross wind made me very conscious of not losing Kazuhiko's luggage as I started rummaging through it.

I managed to find a pry bar. I pulled it out, and closed the boot. I swiftly slung it at the invaded hook but missed. I swung again, connecting this time. The pry bar latched onto the hook. We were nearly one-hundred feet away from the pilots, and one closed in fast, as the other pulled away, trying to take us with him.

I knew I wouldn't have had enough force to pull the bar out along with the hook, so I held on to the side of the cycle again and stomped on the bar.

The hook slid out of place, ripping away a thin part of our cycle's metal frame. The biker behind us sped off and was destabilized by the sudden movement; he carried back in the strong wind, barely dodging the steel flying at him.

Kazuhiko looked back, and then did a double take at the damage, yelling, now very audibly "Not my bike!"

He pulled back just before we reached the broadside biker, and Kazuhiko's larger gyrocycle was pulled out of the way, just above him. I looked back, as he was covered in dust and dirt.

Kazuhiko saw a river running along the forest; he decided to follow it so we would be under the tree line, effectively concealing us from site. We settled a few feet off the surface of the water, and Kazuhiko tipped the bike head down, so that we propelled forward along the river; carefully making sure that we kept our acceleration and lift equal. We made sure to maintain this high while accelerating.

He was visibly stressed; he breathed hard and his knuckles were white because of his tight grip on the controls. The river became larger and let into tributary which we didn't follow. Instead we swept into the dried riverbeds we'd seen from Annabeth's deck which where former paths of the river we followed earlier.

The cycles had caught up again. They stayed above us as we rode inside the trench. One pulled in low behind us; he grabbed a pistol from his waist and aimed for our engine.

He managed to fire off a shot before Kazuhiko pulled back and slammed into the smaller ship behind him. The pursuing gyrocycle was destabilized and thrown off course by the collision; the vehicle slammed against the river bed's side and sent him spinning.

The small gyrocycle wasn't destroyed but damaged beyond repair; the pirate was grounded. Ahead of us there seemed to be a wall of falling water.

Ahead, the river forked into three paths. Kazuhiko lined up for the leftmost path, and as we reached the turn, we flung sharply and drifted around the corner, nose to the ground. The pirates were less skilled in motor craft and had to slow down in order to make it around the corner.

The surprising wall of rain water drew closer and the strong storm started pouring directly on us as we entered into it, the heavy thudding rain created mud around the bank of the river, slowly filling it. The shower of rain and some mud from the banks absolutely drenched us, making nervous about falling off of the side. It was hard to hold onto Kazuhiko's wet clothes *and* keep from sliding on the seat.

The river bed began filling more suddenly with water by a few inches a minute. I put my head against his back to shield my face from the rain, and gripped him tighter still.

Visibility had reduced to about twenty-five feet in front of us, and every stump or rock in the riverbed smashed into our bike as Kazuhiko tried to dodge them.

The riders behind us were now grouped up and seemed to be talking to each other. They followed swiftly behind us but disappeared slowly from view.

Suddenly, the rider who had used the chain gun materialized out of the shield of rain, the other caught up and reached out to stop him, but he accelerated away. He was angled to go right over top of us. I tapped Kazuhiko on the back, and he turned to look. It suddenly seemed like a jousting match, as the rider gained on us ever faster. Just as he was about twenty feet behind us, Kazuhiko pulled the yoke back, sending us nose first in the air, and spun the gyrocycle around. Just as the rider went down to avoid us, Kazuhiko aggressively thrust down. The rider just barely avoided us and crashed into the ground. We hung in the air, Kazuhiko looked at the other biker and I looked back at the rider as he skimmed across the muddy river, burying his bike and flinging himself to avoid losing his legs.

The crashed pirate shook his head at Kazuhiko's stunt, the two seeming to conclude a silent truce. We lifted out of the trench. The second pirate hovered over to help his muddy friend. We headed into the forest on the horizon, that shielded us from the rain we dodged trees at a decent speed.

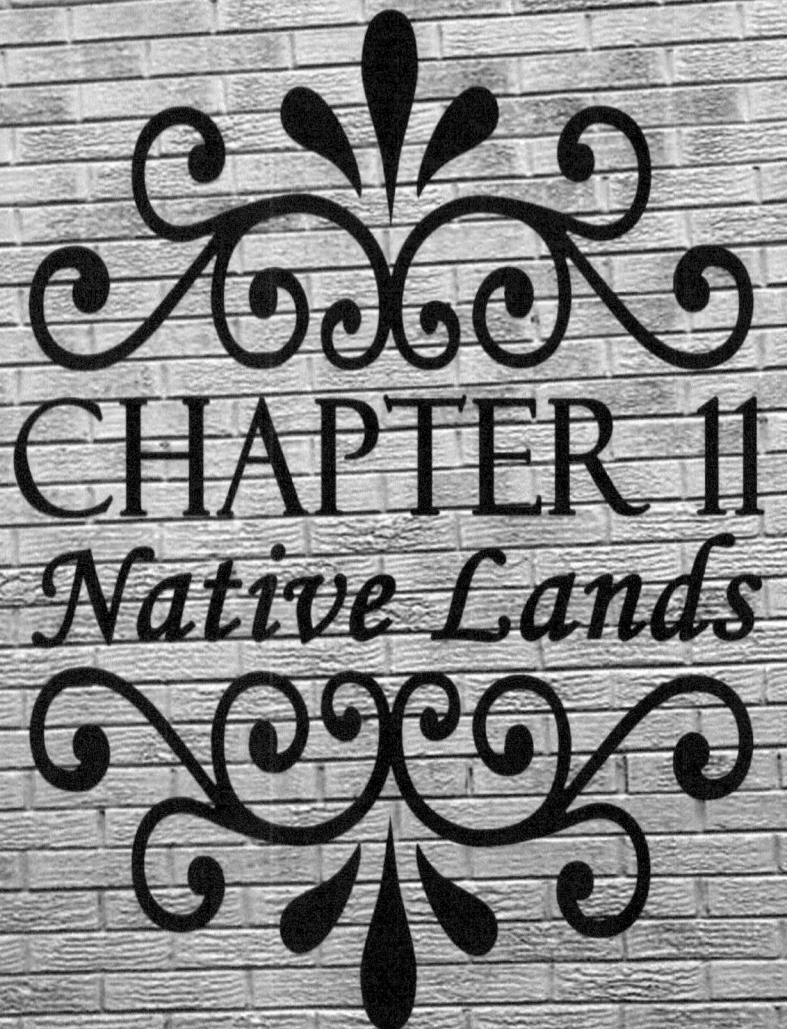

CHAPTER 11
Native Lands

he gyrocycle hit the ground, skipped and skidded to a stop along a shallow muddy river surrounded by a misty Abutyus forest. The bark of the Abutyus tree is like woven bamboo; it stands about ten feet high. The cycle extended landing gear as it lowered in a small enclosed area beside the creek. Kazuhiko jumped off the cycle and splashed in a puddle with a squelch. He examined his soaked wet clothes annoyed at the fact that it was still raining. "This year's Mudan rainfall is the worst." I jumped off as well; my boots got covered in mud. I didn't care too much about my clothes being soaked, because they were not mine to begin with.

He looked toward the trees, his mechanical eye's pupil shrunk then extended, "The Chara is four miles north by foot. We will have to walk through the Abutyus forest." His eyes explored the ground, as he thought. "They rerouted back to the airship..."

"Are they coming back for us?"

"Uh... yes, I'm sure they went to gather more men. We need to be discrete. We should stay low, and not use the gyrocycle. They would be able to spot it miles away."

"How long is it going to take us to get there?"

"Well," He smiled, "that depends on how fast you walk."

"I didn't sign up for this." I said scared.

He laughed. "It'll take longer if you keep complaining. Let's go."

The forest floor was relatively flat, but around each tree were small ecosystems of bamboo, like little hills of vegetation. The Abutyus had wide canopies that blocked most of the downpour, the water was funneled to the areas not covered by the trees and collected on the ground below in small pools scattered across the forest floor.

That was when I remembered something oddly strange about this forest. With some trees, the bamboo had not grown correctly, revealing rough green cacti. We continued on walking in silence which kept my thoughts wandering.

If my dad never left, if my mother stayed with me, I would be home right now. I never pictured my life ending up this way, adventuring through mysterious forests with a prince from a sophisticated country.

I kept wondering what he must have thought about me, and if it were anything interesting. I wanted to ask Kazuhiko all those questions he told me he'd answer, but I couldn't ask him yet, especially because of the rough terrain.

It seemed as we walked, I was concentrated more on the walking, and where to place my feet as to not slip, then the scenery itself.

We stopped at a small clearing between a narrow creek, beside it rested a small hut. The hut was built with bamboo covered in fur to waterproof the sides in a visually appealing way. Bedside it, along a small muddy walkway was a nice dining area also built of bamboo that was lightly streaked with mud from the rain.

As we walked inside, the room was quite quaint certainly like most natives' cottages. The only thing inside was a small stone fireplace, adorned with metal pans and plates on top and in front of it lay a white hide rug.

Kazuhiko walked towards the two chairs which lay against the side wall, and placed them by the empty fireplace. I looked at the floor behind me and thought; *he didn't have to do that for me.*

I sat down; looking at him he seemed happy in that instant. He stood near the side of the fireplace and was looking for something. He started rummaging through a chest. He pulled out a gray fur hide blanket, and covered it around me, which made me blush a little. "Thank you." I said smiling. "How did you know where this place was?"

"My unit built it when we invaded this part of Dekan."

I was confused. "Your unit?"

"They called it Sutirutai; we were trained in desert and forest warfare. The soldiers made us this place and many others like it, when we camped for a battle not far to the east. But those days are long gone. Those people are long gone."

"So, no one will know that we're here?"

He laughed, "Not if we leave soon."

I felt pressured to ask him questions, I had so many of them, but I wasn't sure when to talk. I hated the feeling of not knowing the words to say, or how to go about saying them. He seemed too busy to ask then, because he pulled a wineskin from his messenger bag.

I sat there for a few minutes in silence, thinking about my questions in doubt. *Does he still remember he told me he'd answer my questions?* He handed me the wineskin and asked, "Who else came with you from the orphanage?"

I smiled, "Satomi, and Zilpher my brother."

Kazuhiko laughed a little. "I never heard from Luna that you had a brother; but I guess that doesn't necessarily matter. Now what was it you wanted to ask me?" *My mother never told him?* I was confused, but maybe she didn't like bringing it up. She must have thought he died the day my father was taken. I laid the wineskin on my lap.

"Uhh," I tried to avoid making the conversation less uncomfortable than it was and I talked slowly, only sounding confused if anything. "So if Aruno is your uncle then why…?" I paused, but couldn't think about how to ask him.

"Be careful about what you ask me. I won't leave out any details. I'm guessing you were going to ask; 'why would he lock me up?'" I'm glad he wouldn't leave out any details. But truth is, when he told me this, I couldn't understand what he meant by it.

"Yea," I nodded. "It's doesn't make sense to me. I know you told me before but-"

He cut me off, "What I told you before was the truth. Aruno kept me there because he was afraid I would escape and kill my brother."

"But why would Aruno think that?"

"When I was younger;" He slightly, uncomfortably moved in his chair. "It was after my parents died. I was looking for their will; that was the last thing I had of my parents. Everything else brought back regrets." He paused after that.

I could understand how most things could bring back regrets. When you love someone, then that person passes away, everything becomes reminders of the life that could have happened if they were still alive.

I remembered when my father passed, I hated going near anything that reminded me of him. Those happy days of walking in the marketplace filled me with so much anger I would cry in anguish.

I said remorseful. "I'm sorry to hear that," I hesitated. "If you don't mind me asking, do you know how your parents died? I mean, I've heard stories before but I never knew what to believe of it."

"Don't believe them, the soldiers. Everything you hear from the Raqoian Empire is false. Orfeo killed both King and Queen and they knew it was coming. This century, our countries were never meant to be separated by race."

"Is that what you were taught?"

He nodded, "When Kenzai told me that she was meant to rule, until I married someone from Vermyria, I could not second guess it. Orfeo would never be suited for that position because he seeks only power. If I had only found the will we wouldn't need to be in this situation."

"What happened when you searched for it?"

"My brother didn't like the idea of me looking for it, and he began ordering guards to confine me to my room," He grinned slightly, "but I would always sneak away and I guess he didn't take a liking to that." He carelessly slouched back in his chair, but said nothing, as if he waited for me to ask, "How were you injured?"

"You're referring to my eye I assume. If you really must know; Aruno was at the palace that day when it happened." He moved his hand to his scared face, messing his hair slightly. "My brother did this to me, he figured if I can't see I can't read." At that moment, it was one of the questions I wish I had never asked.

He continued, "He slammed my head into the wall and gouged my eye out." I cringed from the thought. "Aruno tackled him off of me to prevent him from doing any more damage. I'm glad I only lost one eye."

"I…" I wanted to tell him I was sorry, but I didn't know how he would take it. The more I brought up the past, the more he looked hurt, as if his memories were sharp spears digging at him. "Your new eye… It's really intriguing; I've never seen anything like it."

His smile brightened. "That's really nice of you. Aruno hired the Steel Elements to fix my," he paused. "Blemish, in exchange for letting them conducts their strange experiments but... they took it too far. I'm not even sure if they realize what they are doing."

"That... your brother caused that to happen?"

"When you told me why the Raqoian guards were after you, I realized why Aruno came after you when he did. You've ruined Orfeo's only chance at winning over the Vermyrians trust and he's not going to let you forget that."

"Then why are we going straight into the fire by rescuing Kenzai?"

"Because the King will not expect it." He sat forward and held my hand, "I know you're afraid. But Zathena; Aruno and his crew will protect you and although I know Orfeo would enjoy this, he would have to kill me before he could even think about hurting you." As he sat back, he took the wineskin off my lap then continued. "I need to know if she's still alive; and if she isn't... Well, I hope it doesn't have to come to that." I already knew what he would have done. *He'd save Kenzai or die trying.*

"How could I argue with that?" I smiled, "I hope we find her. She's probably been waiting for you for a while now."

The rain outside stopped. But then the sound of heavy rain cycled back through the silence.

"I don't understand. How did Orfeo not get overthrown when he locked her away? Or when he... hurt you?"

"He paid the guards off well and I wasn't there to testify against him. It's truly a pity. Even Luna couldn't help us, and I was for sure she had it under control."

"My mother? How does she know, in fact why was she even on the Annabeth?"

"Well, your mother she… I don't know how to put this delicately." He looked as if trying to hold back a smile. "She stayed with Aruno because she's his uhhhh…Lover?

"What?!" I immediately said muttering. "You can't be telling the truth. Why are you lying to me?"

He laughed, "Did Aruno never tell you?"

"No! She would never marry someone like him! She loved Remington ! I hope you know this isn't funny."

Kazuhiko tried holding back his smile, and kept a straight expression. "Zathena, Aruno married Luna ages ago!"

I was furious, "But, why would my own mother leave me to marry a sky pirate?!"

"Luna did not leave you, she was taken from you. In fact when Aruno saved her, the first thing she asked him, was if he could find you before she left. He might regret that decision now with the ruckus you cause but I can't be angry for obvious reasons."

"Why did she leave? Was it because of him?"

"No one knows where she went, that is why Aruno is so furious. The last thing she told us before she left was 'if you do not hear from me soon, go save my daughter'. Aruno told me that you might have died if he didn't save you.

Not only was the empire after you, but, something or someone else was."

"I don't even know how to feel right now." I stood up, held back my tears and left the hut. *Zathena stop crying. How could any of this be happening?* I ran away from the hut, but the intense rainfall and mist made it hard to see.

The last time I saw my mother she was crying over my father dying. How did she get over this so quickly? Tears started pouring from my eyes. *None of this is possible. What did he mean by someone else is after me? Who could possibly be after me?* What was I to people, when I was only an orphan peasant?

Kazuhiko told me he knew my mother yet she never talked having a son. He must have been lying to me about that. Or maybe she just couldn't remember, but there is no way Zilpher is not my brother. *He's been too nice to me to have lied to me about this.*

He must have been telling me the truth about Kazuhiko! I felt like he was just feeding me information and telling me what I wanted to hear. *But how is that so, when he talked so sincerely.*

I kept running but halted after I realized how far I had ran; when I stopped, the rainfall was so intense I could barely see a mere three feet in front of me. All the trees seemed to have disappeared as well as the hut. The rain poured heavily.

I lost all security having no one to trust and I nowhere to run. Although I didn't know where to go, I was glad it was raining because it washed away the tears.

Why does Aruno deserve my mother's love? I don't trust him. There was no way he could be sincere enough to actually call my mother his 'wife'.

Thinking I heard faint voices, I walked a bit further and found a slight hill flourishing with full grown trees. *Where am I?* I couldn't walk further, I felt scared not knowing which direction to go.

The moment when rain felt cold on my skin, almost freezing; I saw a silhouette that walked in the distance. Than another one, and one last one. I hid behind a tree, the faint voice became clear.

A disembodied toneless voice spoke, "Where do you think the cycle came from?"

Another disembodied one, his voice laughable. "Who knows, the gyros advanced technology looks far more superior then most natives." He laughed.

This one, a girls, "Stop talking we need to find it."

"Who can find anything in this weather?" The older of the two boys said with sarcasm. They were walking closer which caused me to panic.

"Did you hear that?" At first I didn't quite know what he was talking about but as I glanced down I had noticed that my right leg slid slightly in the mud. The rest didn't believe him as he walked slowly, pulling a small knife out of a metal sheath.

"Not this again, who are you going to fool with that!" He walked closer to where I stood. Trying to keep hidden I swiftly and quietly moved behind another tree, apparently in a vain effort.

"Ah HA!" he yelled, "I knew I heard something!" I stood up quickly, vexed and turned to face the kid. He wore some ragged knightly costume and cloak with the Imperial seal branded on the front.

He wasn't very tall for what seemed him being 16. He had a small face structure, and thin nose. His ears were more outward than in, and if anything, his back slouched when he stood. Overall, he looked younger than his intended age.
I pretended to not be annoyed when saying, "Uh... Hello."

"What are you doing out here?" The girl questioned. Her eyebrow raised. She was tall and skinny but looked a bit rough around the edges. Her hair pulled back in a loose bun. She too wore the Imperial seal on what looked like a ragged tunic covering chainmail.

"Oh, I'm just going out for a stroll." It was easier to lie around these unintimidating guards for some reason which felt weird considering how I grew up afraid of them.

"All this way from the city? That's a long distance to only be strolling through." The oldest of them, was a tall average looking teen with watchful eyes. He was dressed in a light leather studded tunic and bow which strung on his shoulder. As I was about to say something, the short kid interrupted me.

"Actually I don't remember seeing you around the village."

I felt panicked, my mind searching for an answer but to no avail. "Well you see..."

"Oh, there you are." I turned around flabbergasted, Kazuhiko stood meters behind me, at the bottom of the small hill. I didn't think he followed me but at that moment I was glad he did.

When I turned back around he walked up beside me and put his arm around me. "Have you squires' met my fine lady?" His statement made me jump, I knew he didn't mean it, but something deep inside made me want to think his words were true.

The group quickly went to bow their heads all except the younger one. "Who is this guy?"

The girl smacked him in the back of the skull, "It's the prince you idiot!" She snapped.

After he quickly realized his social mistake he bowed his head and added in a sarcastic manner, "It looks like you're not the only one with a high opinion of themselves."

She looked nervous, "I'm sorry, he's slow." After which she reminded silent as the older boy spoke.

"What happened to you? Everyone thought your kidnappers killed you!" As Kazuhiko explained what happened to him, he forgot to mention how his abductor was the infamous sky pirate Aruno, his very own uncle! Although I guessed that was intentional. While I stood silent my mind still lingered on the thought of him calling me his.

Then something snapped me back to reality. The storm stopped all too quickly leaving an eerie lingering silence. The cold air tunneled by, causing the hair on my arms to stand on end.

The wind whistled past my ears and swept through my hair. It sounded much like psithurism, or the sound of the wind in the trees piercing my ears. I gaped upward haunted in astonishment, the underside of a huge metal vessel, and red flag fluttering in the clouds.

I looked over at Kazuhiko who, he too was locked in a frightened gaze, agitation visible in his blank expression.

"The soldiers will be so excited to hear about your return!" The girl shouted. He moved away from me, startled by what she told him.

"No!" Kazuhiko became furious; he whispered "You mustn't tell anyone! No one can know that I've escaped or it may lead my captors to my location. I need to be unseen. Does the Chara still belong to Raqoia?"

"Absolutely your highness, the barracks are secretive occupying only us, and our leader."

"Your leader?" He looked surprised. "Tell me, does your leader go by the name, Argo"

He quickly nodded his head, "Viceroy Argo has governed over the natives' land for over ten years!"

"If you will, please lead the way." His rhetorical statement lead to complete understanding of nodded heads and forward walking. The last half of the journey to the native land was made joyous despite the rugged terrain by the groups constant arguing.

The oldest laughed as he playfully shoved the younger boy. "This is Garron if you would like to reprimand him." He said jokingly.

The boy turned to the Prince. "No, you don't understand. Here," As if trying to explain, "Kadon forgot I have amnesia." Kazuhiko said nothing about the statement but laughed.

Kadon yelled in a joking manner, "You don't have amnesia you halfwit!"

Garron added, "Oh yea! A halfwit? I forgot I had that too." I couldn't help but to laugh at that as well.

Kadon was stunned and at first I thought he wouldn't say anything to his simplemindedness. "What?" He laughed

"Stop acting like kids! We are in the presence of royalty."

"Oh, sorry Aunna."

"Uh, excuse me?" I asked.

Aunna turned around, "Yes?"

"How far is the Chara from here?"

"We are just about there!" She laughed.

Just ahead of us was the colossal native's city. Without barriers or tall defense towers. *No wonder this place was so easily taken by Raqoia.* Visibly similar sculpted beasts layered the massive roofs of houses. Trees towered over the streets, creating shelter from both sun and rain.

Vegetation floated on the top of rivers and streams which surrounded the city, and flooded over sidewalks. The grand structures of the Chara stood untouched by forgotten past years, imposing in the sky.

I remembered the beautiful pictures from the books I've read, and noticed it looked nicer in person. Hundreds of Vermyrians' walked in the streets. Some stood talking. Guards stood near buildings with the same menacing helms.

I quickly said without thinking, "You'll be noticed."

Kazuhiko sighed, "I had no idea how many soldiers would be here."

Aunna scuffed her foot in the mud. "Yea, they have been showing up more recently."

I looked at her. "I'm guessing you don't know too much about knightly affairs."

"Not as much as I need to. No." and with that being said, Garron took his red cloak off and handed it to Kazuhiko. Who then studied it before putting it on.

"At least it's a nice color on you." She said laughing.

"Uhh… Thank you." I slightly glowered at her but then suddenly stopped after realizing so.

Kadon surveyed the city. "The Chara is on the next street. We must have walked too far away from the main road." He walked ahead followed by the other scouts.

Walking through the street it was like we were invisible. No one turned their head to yell, "It's the prince!" and it seemed like the disguise was working.

Until the unexpected happened. We walked near a lounge which immediately I looked away, hoping to not be seen. Sitting at a table much eager to stand was Jeju, bottle in hand. Kazuhiko continued walking onward oblivious to her blocking my path.

"Why did you leave the orphanage?" She sounded angry but looked happy.

"I had too I didn't have a choice." I felt nervous from the confusion, "Why are you here?"

"Taeyeon and I were looking for a new job, something to get us out of the orphanage. The soldiers offered us job benefits so we moved here. We were hired to research the plant life and Devin was hired as the translator." Her smile faded and I noticed she was about to cry. "Zathena, Satomi was hired too, but she's gone up missing."

Kazuhiko now aware I wasn't following him, walked up beside me.

"Oh Jeju," I wouldn't be able to stand seeing her cry. "She's not missing; she left with me and Zilpher."

Her smile grew bright, "Are they here with you now?"

Kazuhiko glanced away from me. "No, I'm sorry Jeju, I need to go." As Kazuhiko and I ran away from her I could hear her yelling out my name in anger.

Walking over to the next street I could see the Chara, which seemed much larger than the pictures. We were almost there and I was glad because all this walking started to agitate me.

In fact everyone looked like they shared the same feelings as me. Most of the natives in the city had dark skin, commonly with white markings across their face.

Some stood slouched near their houses while others stood in puddles with smiles on their faces. A blind woman who stood near her front door showed indignant in her expression as she walked inside. Children ran through the puddles, white marks across their smiling faces'.

I felt an arm on my shoulder, as it shoved me to the ground. "This is all your fault!" He antagonized.

I looked up at him, infuriated as Kazuhiko offered me his hand.

I shouted, "What's wrong with you!" The boy looked annoyed as I was helped onto my feet. Then I remembered who this was. He was the same kid who ran into me at the orphanage. Kazuhiko looked over at me and noticed the irritation in my expression.

"It's because of you the soldiers put us here!"

Kazuhiko snarled, "*She* doesn't control the soldiers."

"Oh yea? After she left, the soldiers interrogated us, and because we didn't tell them where she was they assumed we were hiding her!"

"That does not make sense, she is at no fault. You need to calm down."

He irked, "Who are you?" Then he must have not cared. "Whatever I don't have time for this." He walked away in a fit.

"Are you okay?" Kazuhiko solemnly asked me.

"Yea. I'll be fine." We continued our walk. "Do you really think the soldiers put them here?"

"There's no denying it."

I looked down, "This entire problem is my fault, isn't it?"

"Maybe so, but this would have happened regarding your 'treacherous' behavior or not. My brother can only tax Vermyrians in this city. Natives don't have a money system. They trade whatever they can find."

The boy that had left us ran up behind Kazuhiko and before I could warn him, he pulled the Prince's hood off. Kazuhiko quickly turned around, his mechanical eye adjusted.

"OH God you... eye- it's the Prince... He's a freak!" He yelled stammering. Vermyrians turned their heads in confusion. Kazuhiko grabbed my wrist, and pulled me away from the growing swarming crowd.

We ran forward toward the bottom base of the enormous Chara, groups of civilians behind us. The scout group ahead of us, kept the entry open. His hand felt cold, and he wouldn't let go until we reached the door. "Are you okay?" Kazuhiko asked as we walked inside and down stairs, Kadon locking the door behind us.

"Yea, I'm guessing you weren't the only one in need of a disguise."

He smiled, "I assume so." He then looked away. "Where is Argo? I need to speak with him." Garron nodded his head and proceeded to walk down the hallway, entering through a great wooden door.

Argo walked into the room, "Kazuhiko!" he was an average sized man with scruff on his chin, and short brown hair covered by a cavalier hat. He wore a leather doublet and black boots which folded over at the knee of his black pants.

He looked relieved. "How did you escape from your captors? We thought you were being held for ransom!"

"Well, I wouldn't have been able to escape if it weren't for my dear friend."

For a second I looked down smiling. He was right. If not for me, he would still be in the jail that belonged to the Steel Elements.

He took his hat off, slightly bowing, "I honor you dame, you are truly a hero of the highest rank."

I nodded. "Thank you."

Kazuhiko grinned at me. "Argo I need to talk to you in private, so I can tell you what happened." They proceeded to walk away together.

The Chara's basement was made up of large old dilapidated stones. "Follow me," Aunna walked through a side door. The room consisted of a large table filled with fruits, vegetables and seafood platters in the center.

"How did he get discovered?" Aunna asked.

"A group of kids from my orphanage now live in the city."

"That doesn't explain-"

"One of them ran into me and I was accused of relocating them here."

"If the royal highness just escaped from his captors, how were you with him?"

"This is a really long conversation I'd rather not discuss."

Kadon walked inside, carrying plates and empty goblets. "What would you like to eat? Aunna cooked everything!"

"Alright, thank you!" I shoveled only seafood on my plate, meat is something I never really get. Aunna layered her plate with vegetables and fruits.

As I began eating Aunna leaned slightly over the table. "You know, the prince is actually kinda cute." Her statement made me slightly cough. I set my fork down, looking cross. Kadon noticed his sister's peculiar behavior. Aunna smiled, "I'd really like to get to know him more."

Just as I was about to say something the dark room became flooded with red light. I looked out the side window, and saw sparks arcing through the sky.

CHAPTER 12

Chase

$\mathcal{I}$ stood up, frightened by what I was seeing. Kazuhiko yelled in anger, "I told you no soldiers! My brother was never meant to know I was alive!" He came running down the hall, and as he picked up the cloak he looked at me, "Come on we have to go."

I regretted not having the time to rest. I silently muttered, *there was no doubt this was going to happen.* I ran to meet up with him as he threw open the door to the dark city streets. Rain came pouring again, making the roads glisten. Sirens screamed through the town, echoing from the sky. As I looked around, I found no source.

Then, right through the clouds the same airship that flew over us in the forest was descending creating a wake of disrupted rain. As I slowed down, I could see the empire flag fluttering in the sky.

Kazuhiko pulled me by my wrist and lead me into the nearest alley. "Zathena, the empire is more capable than what you understand; try not to worry about it." I shook my head; it was difficult to cope with what was going on. "We need to get out of this city fast." He urged.

He looked away from me, and at that moment he noticed a tunnel of light searching the street we had just left. He grabbed my hand as we bolted away, running down a number of side streets.

The search light followed in our general direction which caused me to panic. The beam of light created by the airship aimed at us from an angle.

As we kept away from the light by hiding in the building's shadows, the light circled overhead. We ran behind the nearest wall hiding from the ray of light.

The powerful beacon lit up the street in front of us and when Kazuhiko whispered, "We run across after the light passes." I agreed and waited.

The light flashed off to a different part of the city and we jumped into a sprint, bolting towards the other side. Then, about halfway across the street the sky lit up again, this time more in a warm yellow like a struck match glowing through the sky.

I felt tremulous waves from a loud explosion, it pushed us sideways enough to make me stumble, and I quickly turned towards the light thinking we might have been fired upon. *Did they fire at us?* I couldn't think of a reason to why they would want us dead.

I stood up quickly, almost fainting from blurred vision. I peered at the explosion, and to my surprise the Annabeth had swung in parallel to the soldiers' airship, firing a volley from its side cannons.

I gapped at the disaster. The giant rounds smashed through the empire's ship, through their engines and its main rigid floatation gas container.

The front nose of the vessel drifted downward causing it to descend. As it picked up speed the wind ripped men off the deck and threw them into the sky.

A reverberation and rumbling echoed through the town as the soldier vessel crashed in the forest forming a rut the length of two ocean liners. It grounded to a stop and, ever so luckily, survived the crash.

After the sound of the crash faded, the screams of thousands of people took its place. Almost as in sequence a vast flame blasted through the ship's engine leaving scorches in the ship's side.

Seconds later, a prodigious column of fire jutted from the sides of the ship. Flames snaked their way across the side and to the hole in the gas container and almost instantly, the whole ship disintegrated under an absolutely massive explosion, lighting the whole town as if it were broad daylight again.

I could feel the heat on my face from where I stood. I looked away from the ship as the second explosion faded and replaced by even more deafening screams.

Kazuhiko could not believe what he saw; he stood shocked for a moment. Perhaps for him this counter attack was unexpected.

I searched the bright sky and noticed a swarm of glinting hornets coming from the massive hull of the Annabeth. The threat from the soldiers' ship had been replaced by a new hazard.

"What are those things?" I exclaimed. "Are they after us?" I said without discerning I had questioned.

Kazuhiko quickly looked at me, recovering his poise and said. "They're on esoteric metallic hovering bikes I think those might have been the strange containers in the hanger. It seems back up has finally arrived. We must hurry."

We finished running hastily to the other side of the street without faltering. I noticed how close we were to the edge of the city; the homes around us beheld an indigence state.

The homes were made from clay and tin roofing. Most of the homes doors were absent, in their place cloth hung, swaying in the violent force of the wind.

The dilapidated homes were hovels in the streets. Some slumped over into the ground, creating piles of rubble in the alleyways. We ran past the homes, jumping over rubble and mucks of trash which covered the streets. The smell of this side of the city was putrid and could knock out a bison.

A growing high pitched whir began sounding through the city; reverberating across the tin roofs, and causing dusty debris to descend from the clay buildings. It was deafening and made it to where I couldn't tell what direction the sound could have been coming from. The hoverbikes held a source of light, but I couldn't pinpoint the exact location.

Kazuhiko suddenly stopped meters ahead of me, placing his hand on his forehead. "Kazuhiko!" I said, as he quickly looked around for something. His gaze laid upon a glinting light reflected on the crest of a tin roof.

Before I comprehended what the light could have meant, Kazuhiko dived through a nearby cloth doorway. As I nervously ran after him, a hoverbike flew from behind one of the taller towers had arched up over the shacks. A beam of blinding light was almost on top of me, and for a moment I stood shocked from fright.

Quickly, I snapped out of it and ran behind a rusted cast iron fence with tin roofing soldered on, but I knew I was not fast enough. The hoverbike seemed to follow me, illuminating the area I was in.

The bike sounded deafeningly close and I could feel the strong downdraft from the tri-rotors above me. *I knew he saw me.* The light slowly dimmed away as the loud rotors faded. *Is he leaving?*

I could still hear the machine, and when I looked up I noticed it was far above me, with its light off in another distance from the slums. I knew I couldn't have fallen too far behind Kazuhiko.

I took the opportunity handed to me, and ran low to the ground from my cover to the doorway he had gone through. Just as I was about to enter the home, I heard one of Aruno's goons shouting. "I saw someone!"

It didn't occur to me that he could have seen Kazuhiko and not me. I kept telling myself. *I can't get caught.* I quickly searched through the home and found muddy foot prints. As I followed them, I could hear rotors winding down which lead me to believe they had landed nearby.

On the other side of the house, I found another cloth doorway fluttering in the wind. His prints seemed to end at the doorway, which suggested he might have gone out that way. I quickly pulled the cloth back, searching the reflective wet cobblestone streets to see if it was safe. Debris from old houses covered the street in front of me, but nothing else. It was like the residents fled from town.

In the center of the street was a moss covered well, circled by many houses. I ran quickly through an alleyway leading to the well.

Behind me I heard a man running; I looked over my shoulder and saw him sprinting full tilt after me through the wet alley. I looked around at the homes and found an open door that the prince might have ran through.

After noticing that the man behind me looked to be the hoverbike pilot, I made my way into the house.

As I closed and locked the door, I heard the man "uhff" as he slammed into the door. I swiftly picked up the chair next to the door and barricaded it shut. "Zath!"

No! I knew it was Sir Jonny. I had hoped it would be some other dashingly sky pirate, maybe one not so talented. *I know this won't hold him back for long.* I thought to myself as I turned the corner.

In the darkness of the room I could see movement. I almost blindly entered into the next room, when I noticed a husband and wife with three kids sitting in the corner behind a fabric covered hay bed. Their eyes were slightly glimmering in the dark, disturbance painted on their faces.

"I know you're frightened, I'm so sorry." No reply, only blank expressions. I could faintly hear Sir Jonny saying his coordinates presumably into a communication device of some sort. Then I heard him kick at the door.

"Can you please tell me which way the man went?" I whispered, as if speaking lower would conceal my location longer than it had.

The little boy of the three walked over to where I stood, baffled as if to reconsider if I were a dream. He pointed at the archway behind me and whispered barely audible, "Out that way." I jumped as a second kick was heard and the door frame cracked. The little boy screamed and ran into the arms of his frightened mother.

I ran into the next room and suddenly a light flashed through the window. I ducked behind the kitchen cupboard as another hoverbike raced by. I knew it had come to back up Sir Jonny.

I ran further out a door that had not been fully closed. Down the alley to the right, the road ended by a large brick wall. The road was covered by an old long stone loggia. Visible doors unopened, still locked shut. Kazuhiko must have gone the other way, and upon turning to the left, I heard a hoverbike zoning in but the direction was uncertain.

The sound of wood cracking and being smashed came from behind me.

"Where did the girl go?" Sir Jonny was outraged. *I'm not going to stay around for this.* I told myself. I doubled my pace toward the end of the alley.

Close to the end of the pathway, the bike swooped sideways in front of me, and pulled up at the last second so it wouldn't hit the building. This had the effect of pointing the rotors at the alley, and a large quantity of air jettisoned in my direction creating a wind tunnel.

The air threw me back and to the ground and I skidded across the slippery road, mud staining my clothes. I stood up quickly and backed away from the new threat.

I turned around; contemplating on finding a new door to run through when I saw Sir Jonny come out of the house I had left. *I knew this was going to happen.* I couldn't find another way out it had seemed.

I knew why Kazuhiko left me behind, he used me as bait to help him leave undetected. *It couldn't have hurt to tell me that before dragging me along.*

Sir Jonny sprinted toward me, his feet splashing in the rain inaudible over the loud hover machine behind me. I flinched frightened as he grabbed me by my arm, muscle fatigue caught up with me, there was no way I could manage fighting him off.

He pulled out handcuffs, grabbed my arms and pulled them in front of me, slapping the restraints on my wrists. The pirate on the hoverbike floated there for a moment, waiting for orders. He then flew off after Sir Jonny had told him to search for Kazuhiko.

The bikes rotors blew wind into our faces and through my long hair.

Sir Jonny lead me to where he had parked his vehicle. That's when I should have ran and forgot about the consequences of leaving for the second time; but I had already tried that, and I already failed trying.

I decided it would be better leaving with Sir Jonny than trying to find Kazuhiko, one who would already be gone, untraceable. He had left me here, as bait, it hurt he didn't tell me, but what can I expect from not asking him when I had the chance.

He smirked. "You shouldn't run off like that again. It's not safe." If I didn't feel like walking I sure didn't feel like arguing. All my mind kept thinking about was what Aruno would say, and even though it wouldn't bother me, I still thought about it.

CHAPTER 13
Disagreements

*T*he new hover cycles were something straight out of fantasy. They shone with new metal I had never seen before like patterned steel. The bottoms of them lit up with an eerie dim blue glow. There were three rotors, two smaller ones in the back and a larger one protruding from the front. They looked to be like small airship engines on the side to give the vehicle faster forward acceleration.

The back had a seat for a passenger rider, but as I sat down, I realized it was not for a passenger but rather a prisoner. He clicked a button behind my seat causing a mechanism to go over the chain between the cuffs and it then pulled down to the body of the bike locking me there. Then, by clicking another button a metal belt circled around my waist, latching to the back of the seat so I couldn't fall off.

The way Sir Jonny carried himself, was sure-footed. He flipped a few switches before putting the key in the ignition. After he turned it, the bike slightly lifted but then fell and went out with a spur. He muttered something in Raqoian and too quietly to understand.

He opened a small panel and pulled out a cylinder filled with what looked like lightning, and after pulled a second one from his pocket, slamming it into the socket. He turned the key again and the turbines spurred to life. In about five seconds the rotors spun up to speed and we lifted off, the city spread out below us. We whipped about and aimed for the Annabeth.

I looked below and saw the fire from the Imperial airship stretching out. The screams from the lost souls now vacant, lost. They had all died, I knew no one survived. Sir Jonny looked behind him, "Do you understand what happens when we agree to the prince leaving? Five-hundred people, all dead; and you let it happen. This is because of you."

My voice stayed silent. He was right, *I* let the prince go; *I* was noticed, and *I* was the reason a soldier airship flew in. However, I would not be blamed for killing them. I wasn't the one who had fired the cannons. I was not a murderer with blood on my hands, and I wasn't going to let them tell me otherwise. I felt anger build up inside of me, and for the first time my tears fell silent.

The hoverbike leaned in the direction of the Annabeth and accelerated quickly. Our location, about two miles away and we approached fast. The rain started again, pelting our faces, and washing away my tears. Sir Jonny quickly put on goggles and increased the altitude.

When we hit the clouds, the moisture soaked our clothes, and after rising above them, we ascended into the dark starry sky.

Below me, the town had disappeared, replaced by a rolling ocean of black clouds. We soon caught up to the

Annabeth, and Sir Jonny called in on a communication device housed in the control console. "I've got her." The reply was Raqoian and muffled behind a stark static.

We swooped under the canopy of the balloons and descended into the hanger. Sir Jonny pressed a button and the restraints that locked my handcuffs to the ship slid back into its slot, and the belt unlatched itself.

He stepped off the side of the bike and walked up beside me, helped me off and led me into the airship. We past many pirates through the main lobby and all held the look of shame. They looked sorry to know me and they acted as if I were the criminal.

We walked into the library of the ship. I paused. Zilpher was nowhere to be found; a new type of doubt filled me. I thought that maybe he was disappointed with me, for running off with the prince after he told me to be careful. *I don't want him to see me like this. Everyone thinks I'm a criminal, but how can I be.*

I stopped near the archway, and to my surprise, Zilpher was walking into the library. He gaped, "Zathena?"

Before he went in for a hug, I backed away. He looked confused. "Is something wrong? Where have you been?" I said nothing and walked past him and continued to follow Sir Jonny.

He gestured at me to stop near Aruno's room. When I did, he opened the door for me. Upon entering it, he closed the door shut behind me.

Aruno sat in the chair closest to the window. He was looking out at the passing clouds from down below. He obviously knew that upon his door opening, I would be waiting. I felt all of my anger build up inside of me, and as he turned around, it was like a bomb went off.

"How could you kill all of those innocent people?!" I shouted; my voice strained with anger. He looked shocked at my outburst, but somehow prepared.

He stood up, "Innocent?" He sounded baffled with rage. "They have blood of thousands of innocent people on their hands! And you have the audacity to call *them* Innocent?"

"How could you possibly know how many innocent lives they stole?"

He looked as if I were crazy to ask such a question, "Because, *I* used to be the general for the Raqoian army. I know what it takes for them," He abruptly stopped, and paced around the room before changing the subject. "That's not the point. The point is they were coming to arrest Kazuhiko and imprison you for harboring a refugee. Then probably get as much information out of you about my whereabouts as possible. Then that's it, they wouldn't need you any longer;" He began to tear up from anger, "and I can't lose you like I lost your mother."

"I thought you told me you didn't know my mother!"

He smirked. "Don't act like Kazuhiko didn't tell you everything. He could never get over the stories your mother used to tell him. Or the photographs she kept of you." I felt my face relax from the anger I had built up. Kazuhiko did like me back then. Does that mean he loves me now that he's met me? Did he mean what he said when he told them I was *his*? *No! That can't be right,* I told myself.

I looked at Aruno. "Will you please get these things off of me?" I questioned, while moving my restrains in an outraged manner.

He walked over to me with a key in his hand. "You need to calm down-,"

"Did you love my mother?" I interrupted while he unlocked the handcuffs around my wrist. A question not needed to be asked I later found out.

"I love her more than life itself," A smile appeared across his face, his visible scar creased. This may have been the first time I saw him smile near me, "She's my everything; I would die for her if I had to."

"That doesn't make sense, if you love her then why did you lie to me about knowing her?"

Aruno walked back behind his desk and sat down in his leather chair.

"I needed to rescue you from the empire, lying to you was my only option. Once it worked I had to deceive you further because I'm not quite sure where she is. It was better to dash your expectations then, then to keep you guessing; and after her attempt to save the princess failed, she vanished. Zath, there's no easy way to say this, she could be dead."

"I never got the chance to know her!" I welled up in anger, unaware of my absent tears. "If she told you to come find me why did you wait so long? What was the point in finding me *after she left*?

"I had no choice in the matter. If I had helped you earlier, I could have led them to your location." I calmed down then, for the most part.

"What do you mean? Kazuhiko told me the same thing. Who could possibly be after me?" Aruno looked away for a moment. "There are people looking for you Zathena." He scratched his head and looked as if he didn't know how to continue the conversation. "You're right; I should have found you earlier, it would have been much easier keeping you safe." He looked at me, "they may have already found you. However, I'm not quite sure. I can't trust a lot of people on this ship seeing that a lot of them came from the empire. That's why I hired people to keep it under control, like the Steel Elements."

"Is that because... you can torture the people you mistrust, without actually doing the deed yourself?"

"That is exactly right."

"So... Avner? He was one of them, wasn't he?"

Aruno nodded. "He was unique enough to follow me, steal my key himself and convince you to break the rules. However he was not smart enough to actually think I would believe you to be mistrusting. I knew of his plans the moment I found my door unlocked, and the key misplaced.

No one on this ship would be dumb enough to break the only two rules I have enforced time and again." Not only had I felt annoyed then but I felt offended.

"But, how could you be certain that I was the one to break the rules?"

He grinned, "You are a very curious child." I stood thinking for a minute, rubbing my arm.

"What if, instead of me, it was my brother?"

"Tell me, do you sincerely believe Zilpher is your brother?"

I looked away, and paced toward the side of the room. I truly don't know why I did this. I stopped in front of a mirror and just stared at the frame of it as I played with a ringlet of my long hair.

"I don't know what to think, but when I think about it... I don't know honestly." I picked up a gold piece that was sitting on the frame. "I remember a child running away from my home after my father was murdered, but I vaguely remember him and I have no photos of us together."

"I never believed him to be your brother from the beginning." I stuck the gold piece in my pocket as I turned back around facing Aruno. "Your mother never mentioned having a son, she either only loved you or he never existed." Aruno picked up a few parchment papers from his desk and reviewed them. "I let him come here with you because I needed to keep an eye on him. Shortly after he arrived, we sent him to training. For a kid who grew up on the streets, for some reason we don't understand, he was as skillful as a soldier in combat and could fend off any one of my men."

"That's... not right." Aruno stood from his desk. "He was lying to me this entire time." I looked down, "He was so nice to me, and it doesn't make sense."

He continued, as he walked to the front of his desk "There is a possibility he could be telling you the truth." At that time, it sounded like he had only said that to make me feel better. As if he was trying to tell me that being lied to sometimes happens and that, I shouldn't feel bad over it. "Your mother couldn't quite remember everything about her past." He shifted the conversation, as he leaned back on his desk, arms crossed. "However, I think you should have the right to know, he has lied to you before."

"What could he have lied to me about?" I found myself rubbing my arm again.

"The elder from the marketplace, was never discriminated against by the Raqoian guard. For some unknown reason, he lied to you."

The memories kept circulating through my mind. The pictures of my family. The stories of my father. The little boy running from my home. "How do I know who to trust?"

He exaggerated, "I'm Raqoian. However, Zilpher on the other hand?"

"Something isn't right, why would he lie to me about that? What could he possibly gain by lying to me about someone being discriminated against?"

Even if he isn't my brother and can never be. Even if the child that ran away from my home wasn't who I was led to believe; why would I be lied to about this? Nothing seemed to make sense to me.

"Good question, something that I don't even have an answer for. He is older then you Zath, your mother would have told me about her first born son. She would have loved him more then you just for the fact of him being alive longer." My mind began to clear. *Aruno's telling me the truth.* When I think about Zilpher he doesn't look too familiar.

I was blinded by his kindness.

I still needed more proof. Something deep inside of me kept telling me that maybe he was confused about this whole thing. *He was confused.* Just like that, my ability to think was altered. I couldn't picture him as my brother anymore; it would have never made sense to have a brother.

All of the things my father ever told me about the love he had for me, came flooding back, as if I had kept it locked away until the most inconvenient time. *"I love you Zath,"* He would say every night after reading me to sleep-which I faked one night just out of curiosity. *"Having a son couldn't compare to the happiness you've given me."*

"Aruno, you… you're right. I remember now, my father… He never mentioned having a son."

"You're just now remembering this?"

"I…" I stuttered, "It wasn't really a part of my life that I… wanted to remember. Can you rightly blame me for not remembering? It was a time when my father was murdered. When I was young I dealt with things by pushing them behind me, I had to move forward or I would have been stuck in the past. These years I have to focus on the now to survive, the past seemed not near as important." I felt like I was rambling on-and-on about my life; I hoped he understood what I meant because on something's I didn't.

"I wanted a friend more than anything else, I thought... Zilpher understood me. It seemed more reasonable, useful and helpful for him being my brother than it was for him to be lying" I looked up at him. "Aruno, he had proof to, at least to me, because he knew the story of my parents. He knew their names and... the date my father died."

"Anyone could have found that information through the cities obituaries but whoever would let a child look through the archives is really beyond my comprehension."

"When I was younger and dreamt about living here, on this airship I mean. I always pictured being able to make my own decisions and having the freedom to come and go as I please. Now living here, I've realized that's never going to be the case. I know I can't leave, but I don't want to be here anymore because I feel threatened."

"Zath if you stay on the airship, nothing can harm you."

"You can't guarantee that!"

As he hugged me he sincerely said, "I'm sorry I put you through all this." To me, his words sounded sarcastic.

I shoved him away from me, "Don't touch me!" I backed away. "You love my mother and I respect you for that, but I will never respect you enough to call you my step-father."

I left the room, and right after I heard Aruno lock the door behind me. I walked across the hallway to my bedroom; I wasn't in the mood for eating food or talking to anyone. Sleep was the only thing on my mind that I could care about at that time. When I entered my room and laid in the softness of my bed, I felt the heaviness of my eyes close and I immediately fell asleep.

I was shaken awake by a cloudy figure which loomed over me. "Zathena, run, hide!" Were the only words that could escape the mouth of the hazy figure. I bolted behind my bed, but something wasn't right. Everything was so vivid, yet I couldn't feel the floor nor the walls. The figure in from of me, blurred out of sight.

A loud crashing noise erupted from the hallway; and as I looked, the door to my bedroom was missing. A door frame was all that was left. A figure leaned struggled on the door post. Blood dripped from his clothes and onto the floor. I heard screams and explosions. I was steadily shocked and as I looked above my bed I saw that it was Orfeo, the left side of his face was bleeding; and he cackled with a grin. "I won."

I screamed as I woke up, and my eyes were burning. Satomi was sneaking into the room as I sat up.

"Zathena?" She questioned with a whisper as she quietly shut the door behind her. "Did you have another night-scare?"

"More like night-terror," I said as I slid my feet toward my stomach, laying my arm over them. I briefly yawned, "What time is it?" Satomi walked over to me, baffled by my question.

"Midnight around twelve; how does this even matter? Why did you run off with the prince without at least telling me?"

"I didn't want Aruno knowing."

"You think I would have been the one telling him? Everyone found out that you were missing as soon as the pirates arrived back."

I laughed nervously, "How angry where they?"

"This is nothing to laugh about. Zilpher feared the worst; and Aruno... I've never seen a person so angry before."

"He killed those people, Satomi."

"They were going to kill you, without even thinking about it."

I sighed. "I went with Kazuhiko because he told me he would tell me who I truly am. I was done guessing, so I snuck out." I pulled my hair over my right shoulder, brushing through dusty portions with my fingers. "He told me Aruno is married to my mother. That he's my..." I could not get the words out because I didn't want to. I hated just thinking about it.

"Your step-father?" Satomi looked fairly shocked. "He never seemed to act like one,"

"Yea." I interrupted. Satomi's eye brow creased. I interrupted her before she got her point across, which annoyed her.

"All except for the fact that he protected you; about a dozen times." At the time I thought, *of course he protected me in situations that would have never happened if I never came here.* Then I just stared at her for a moment, continuing my thoughts. So many things happened to me through the last couple of days every situation was blending in with each other. He told me not to go through the white door but I did. I let the prince out and caused a mess all because I wanted to leave. *What have I been thinking?* He's been helping me this entire time.

"I guess you are right..." My legs were sore as I stood up and I noticed my clothes were dusty from the journey earlier. "He still killed those people though..."

"He had his reasons." Satomi put her hand on my shoulder. "He was trying to save you."

"Well, what if they never would have arrested me to begin with? What if they were just after the prince, and not me?"

"You know the chances of that happening right?"

I sighed, "Alright, well I'm going to freshen up a bit before falling asleep. Could you bring me some clothes in later?" Satomi nodded as I walked into the bathroom.

Upon removing my clothes I found a gold coin in my pocket and realized it was the one I took from Aruno's room. I can't believe I had forgotten about this until now. I laughed to myself. I knew I had to return it. I wouldn't have felt right keeping it. I've never had a feeling like that before. I felt as though I didn't want to disappoint him; but then again maybe that is only because I couldn't stand getting in trouble again. Not for what this is worth.

Satomi brought a medium lengthen laced white cotton nightgown and set the rest on a small side table near the tub. "Did you and Aruno have a fight when you came back?"

"I told him I would never call him my step-father."

"We are one step closer to finding your mother. We have been this entire time. I feel like, even if you dislike him, or we end up hating him for one thing or another. You should at least act like you respect him. Who knows? Maybe his personality will change toward you, and then you will love where we ended up."

I scrubbed my leg. "You're right; this might be the best opportunity I have had so far, and I keep screwing everything up-"

Satomi interrupted me. "No you didn't! If it weren't for *you* we wouldn't have been adventuring as much as we had. When I found out *you* were the one who told the king off *and* started a riot? I was steadily impressed. You have the guts to stand up to anyone. I wish I was more like that."

I laughed. "I would have never said anything to Orfeo if I had just thought about it first. I didn't know I'd be in this much trouble."

"It's enjoyable." Satomi said excitedly. "If you can really help prince Kazuhiko, you'd be known as a Hero all throughout the two kingdoms. All Vermyrians will be free from Raqoia and love you as a result!"

"I want to help him; but how can I? He was looking for the princess when I went with him, but I blew our cover. I don't know how I can help him find her now."

"I'll help you next time! We will find your mother and Lady Kenzai together! All four of us, including your brother."

"There's something I need to tell you about that." Satomi looked a bit confused she tilted her head, "About what?"

"Zilpher isn't really my brother. I think he must have been confused. I remembered recently that, my father never told me I had a brother. One night he told me that all the happiness I brought him could never measure up to having a son. And that he was okay that I was the only daughter he had."

"That is so strange. He is still our friend right?"

"Well, that I don't know because there's something not right about this entire thing. I'm sure I need some time to think about it."

"I think I do too." Satomi's attention went to the floor. "Hey, what's this?" She picked up the gold piece that lay on my dirty clothes.

I almost felt nervous but then stopped myself. "I accidently took that from Aruno." I couldn't quite help myself from laughing. "I'll return it later."

Satomi laughed a little, "You kleptomaniac."

I continued laughing because it was true, almost. "Hush up!" I threw water at her and she stood up. "Oh, hey! Don't get your filth water on me!" She laughed as she opened the door. "Gross."

She was right. We are one step closer to finding my mother; and it's all because I was so naive. Although I was sure that Aruno would have found me either way. I'm not quite sure I would have gone with him if the soldiers never came to the orphanage.

*   *   *   *   *

As I walked up to Aruno's room some pirates walked behind me through the hallway. "That's the girl?" I looked over my shoulder. Long black straggly hair put up in a pony tail. His jaw was defined by the scruff of his beard. His clothing was like an eastern privateer.

The other looked like he had a nasty case of scurvy. His skin was pale as a ghost and when he talked I noticed gaps where his teeth should be. "Yea, shocking, isn't it?"

The first guy laughed, "Aruno picking favorites."

As they walked away I heard the ending trails of their conversation. "Do you think changing our flag confused the Raqoians?"

"Absolutely not."

The pale man laughed, "Yea, Orfeo would have known." After that they left into the control room.

I knocked on Aruno's door but after a minute of silence I decided to turn around and head back to my room.

Right before I turned around, I heard the door unlock. I slightly jumped as he opened the door. He stood in his pajamas which consisted of only pants. "Uh," I stood there for a moment then casually asked, "Did I wake you?"

"Believe me; your delicate knocking couldn't have woken a lamb. Did you have a nightmare?"

"Somewhat more of a headache then anything, but that's not why I'm here. Look I'm sorry about what I said earlier. You've helped me and saved my life a couple of times; and I normally don't say this too many people; but, thank you. I'm glad that you helped me."

Aruno's smile quickly faded. "You're welcome; but it's not that big of a deal. Anyone who knew about your situation would have done the same."

I pulled the gold coin out from my pocket. "I uh… took this by accident."

"Whoa," Aruno looked shocked as he took the coin from me examining it. "I'm surprised."

"Really?"

"No, I noticed you took it when you held it in your hand. You still need to work on that."

"It's not something I want to critique."

He handed the coin back to me, "Keep it, it was your mothers. It has her initials carved in it."

I smiled. "Thank you." I nodded my head as I was about to turn away.

"Oh, and one more thing." I hadn't quite turned away yet, and I glanced back at him. "Zilpher is missing." Worry pinned in the crease of his brow. "We've examined every cabin of this ship. He has simply disappeared. We don't know where he could have gone." I couldn't tell if he were lying, or telling me the truth. I've never seen him with this expression before.

"uh… I haven't seen him either."

Aruno looked down the hall. "If you do happen to see him again, please let me know. You're one I can trust among other people."

"Maybe he will turn up tomorrow."

"Possibly, but until then you should get some sleep," He leaned back and looked as if he were picking something up off of a nearby table. "Here, drink this; it should help with the headache." He handed me a glass of clear liquid.

"What is it?" I thought he might have been handing me vodka or something.

"It's medicine. It's all I have to offer you."

"Uhh…" I looked at the glass. "Okay. Good night."

Aruno smiled, "Good night Zath." And then shut the door as I walked away. I opened my room's door and took a sip of the mysterious drink. It tasted sweet. I walked to my bed and sat down; then took a swig of it before falling asleep.

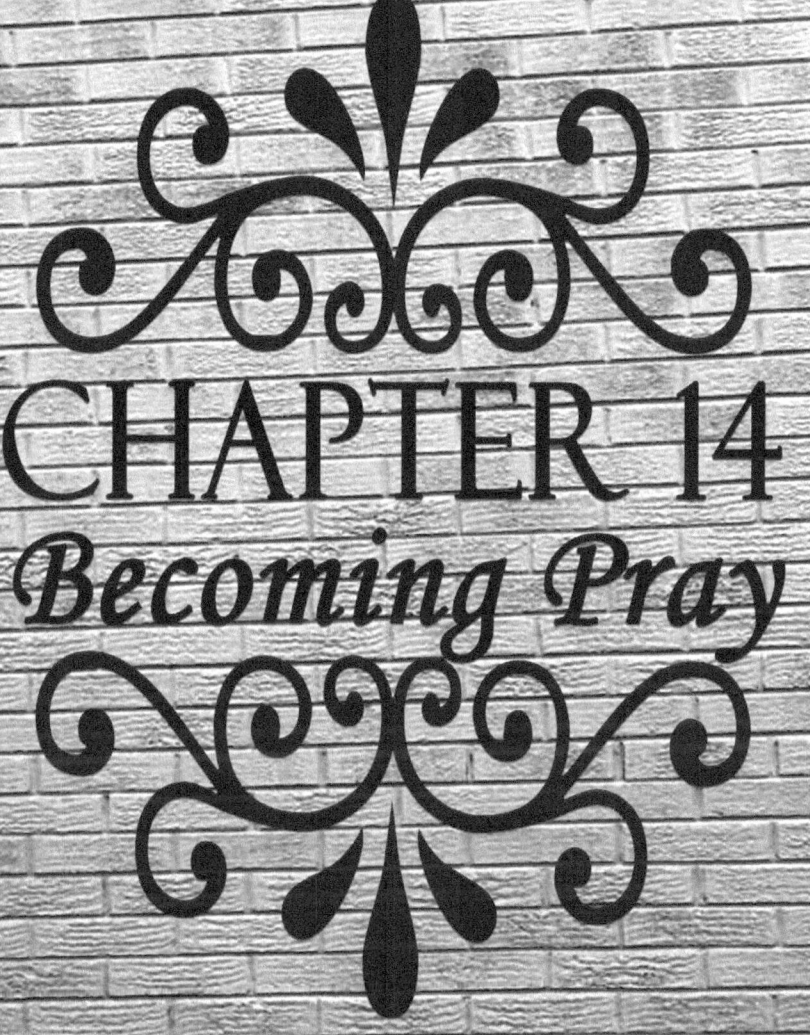

CHAPTER 14

Becoming Pray

I woke up startled by the sounds of metal tearing and wood splintering. I realized last night was peaceful. I slept the entire night restful without being interrupted by nightmares.

Within a few seconds a loud siren rang out throughout the ship. An intercom screeched loud above me, the speaker was non locatable. "We are under attack, repeat we are under attack. There is smoke below deck. Everyone in this location please grab the air purifiers provided. Warriors get to your battle stations and pilots get to the hanger. All non essential personnel get to the armory above deck." The intercom kept replaying after that as if it were on loop. However, it was nearly drowned out by the loud sirens.

A small part of the wall clicked open and a gas mask respirator appeared in the opening. I noticed something different about them. They had small tanks of oxygen hooked to the sides of the front. This was probably for fighting the low air pressure which was helpful to not give them a disadvantage. The door in front of me clicked as locks were being opened automatically.

My door made a low pitch whirl as the locking mechanism turned and the door swung open letting in a small cloud of smoke, which danced across the ceiling. I grabbed my teddy bear which lay on the bed, and ran over to grab a gasmask. I put it on my face and pulled some straps on the back until it was snug. After putting mine on, I grabbed a smaller one which I then pulled over my teddy's head, securing it on tightly.

I quickly left my room and entered into a world of confusion and noise. Men were running every which way. Within minutes the cycling intercom voice stopped, replaced with Melvin's barked mumbling. "We have a hole in the poop deck, and crap is going everywhere!" Loud laughter could be heard around the middle of the ship.

Next I heard a loud clap. Someone had slapped him. Aruno yelled. "Get off of the PA system!" He continued quickly. "A round has pierced the forward cargo bay, there is a fire; anyone nearby, put it out now! The assailant is an Artillery ship spotted three miles at nine o'clock. Pull into her left for a broadsided cannon attack!"

With that the Annabeth swung towards the right and tilted upward at a thirty degree angle. Some people were smart enough to grab a-hold of something to keep them steady, while others tripped and stumbled or just flat out face planted into the decking. I managed to grab the door frame of the room I had just stepped out of.

As the ship leveled out, I could hear a faint smash. A fracture was visible far away from me in the hallway; along the outer wall.

I was baffled, it all happened so quickly. A four foot wide artillery cannon round from the new assailant had smashed the wall along the side of the Annabeth and then ricocheted off. Pirates who had recently came out of their quarters were near the impact point and thrown against the opposite wall. If we had turned late; the artillery-shell would have pierced into the ship and killed all of us.

I had to get to the surface and find Satomi and Zilpher. I knew he had to still be on this ship, but where? What if Aruno lied to me and put Zilpher away? Aruno's worried expression was more than enough to convince me Zilpher was missing.

I ran along the inside wall just in case Annabeth experienced any more sudden movements. I found the surface exit near the other side of the lobby. Loud pistol rounds and other various weapons were being fired from about thirty pirates all lined across the deck. They were firing at nearby flying enemy troops, mounted on an older model of Kazuhiko's bike. This bike had two rotors above the bike with small guns hooked to the front.

Along the side decks of the Annabeth lined anti-aircraft guns and they fired nonstop. One of the enemy's hover cycles were shot down, hit in the drive shaft between its two rotors with an explosive shell. It lost all control and started falling toward the ship; slamming the deck and throwing the pilot over the handle bars.

He was quickly surrounded by three pirates with at least four different guns trained on him. I rushed over to see what we going to happen to this Raqoian soldier. I slipped in between two of Aruno's men.

The crashed enemy soldier had not only survived but was holding a pistol and waving it around in a futile gesture. He shouted over the clamor, "You can't take me! I will never betray the Empire!" And to end his blabbering words the pirates brought their guns to his head. The guy whispered, "I may have changed my mind..."

The pirates pulled the guns hammer back, "Get up," One man pulled him off of his feet and moved him away from me at gun point.

When I looked back up, everyone who was distracted by this man's small speech had run back to the matter at hand of defending the Annabeth against the oncoming attack of Raqoian imperialists.

All of our anti-aircraft guns were fully up and all barrels were firing. Their cycles were forced to back off; but we shot two more down before they could get back to the cover of their ship.

Their Artillery ship looked different from the Annabeth. Its flotation gas containers were attached around the sides instead of suspended above. This gave the large gun that swiveled in the middle, a greater angle to fire.

The Empire ship seemed to have found us on accident and decided that to attack was a better idea than for first calling backup. It was a bad maneuver on their part, seeing that their ship was nearly half our size and had no present close range cannons.

The Annabeth had swooped in fast and their big artillery cannon had a hard time getting a good aim. I thought this had to be because maybe it being a support ship and not meant for engaging enemies at close range had something to do with it. The thought made me laugh. It's not like it stopped them from trying their darndest to put as many holes in our armor as they could.

As the soldiers loaded a new cannon shot, my stomach lurched as we pitched forward the Annabeth taking a nose dive to get below the soldiers ability to aim. In the few seconds that gravity was lost, I tripped slightly and it pulled me five feet forward.

Downward forced pulled at me as I momentarily fell backward. The ship leveled as we got out of the aiming point of the cannon. I pulled my gasmask off to see clearly. We were five-hundred feet away and coming in low. The soldiers were nervously running around to the side of their ship. Firing down at us, but quickly pushed back by our concentrated anti-aircraft fire.

Satomi stood with her back to me, dressed head-to-toe in new gear; and excitedly firing a rifle bigger than she was. She fired at the soldiers causing her to stumble backward; her rifle rose to the sun. She screamed in excitement and jumped as an enemy soldier fell on the opposite ship.

She reloaded and shot again, this time rubbing her shoulder from the kickback.

I ran up to her asking, "When did you become so…"

Her words cut me off, she spoke quickly and solemnly. "I snuck into the armory, don't tell anyone! Here's a gun." She quickly pulled a pistol with five barrels from her side holster. I grabbed it from her smiling and shoved it in my belt pouch's holster. *I know I'd need this later.*

The Annabeth flew back up to be on the imperial ship's side. The pirates started firing at the enemies balloons but instead it penetrated the underside; puncturing holes in the ships armor. Perhaps they weren't quite ready to shoot it down.

Aruno's voice came over the PA system again as he yelled, "Prepare the broadside cannons!"

The soldiers were running below deck to gain as much protection as possible. As soon as the pirates had the right angle position to fire they did so upon Aruno's command. "Fire!"

The guns were deafening. For five seconds, everything on the boat and around it, including the air seemed to shake. A large smoke wall circled in the air and then was swept away by the strong wind around us. The ship in front of me appeared to be a vista of destruction.

The balloons on the back side ripped open. The ones on the other side kept intact and they stayed lifted. The small ship fell vertically into the clouds below. Soldiers that never ran below ship fell off, embracing the sky in a spinning motion. The clouds stretched out below the ship were painted an orange hue. Everything was calm for a few minutes, a weird contrasting quietness after death of over one hundred soldiers.

The tranquil reflective state didn't last for long as the pirate crew got back to work, preparing and restocking weapons. "Hey!" Someone slapped my shoulder, pulling me into a side hug. "Good job at not getting yourself killed." It was that eastern looking pirate who talked about me in the hall.

"Thank you?" I questioned confused and startled.

The Annabeth quickly flew into another cloud layer for cover so it would be hard to spot us at first glance.

He rubbed Satomi's head and messed up her hair. "Be careful you two." He looked at me, "There are bound to be more imperial ships around."As he walked away the ship became enveloped in clouds.

My eyebrows rose, "How old do you think that guy is?" I asked Satomi.

She was still looking in his direction. "It's hard to tell a Raqoians age. He surely can't be older than twenty." She smiled.

"You like him, don't you?"

She held the same dazed smile across her face. "What? No." She shook her head. "I don't even know who he is."

"You're good at this whole, sky pirate thing."

"It's really exciting! Yet, it's frightening at the same time. My stomach is in knots. I think this may have given me battle scars."

"Real battle scars!" I question in a sarcastic tone. "Are you okay?" I asked quickly and perhaps with too much excitement.

"I think I was hit by debris from the deck." She pulled up her sleeve to reveal a number of large and small cuts on her arm. "I'm not going to die or anything. I'll be fine." She laughed light heartedly.

I couldn't believe I almost forgot. "Let's go find Zilpher! I heard he had gone missing. I hope he isn't injured."

"Others told me they feel like this was Zilpher's fault."

"That's ridiculous! You can't believe everything you hear." I looked around through the mist of the clouds placed upon the decks of the Annabeth, but didn't see him.

We ran along the middle of the deck to find anyone who might tell us where he could be. As we ran along we couldn't spot him. We were on our way toward the control center to find someone who might know of Zilpher's whereabouts.

At about twenty meters away from the control bridge the clouds around us dispersed and vanished behind us. Both Satomi and I stopped abruptly at the vista that was then apparent to both of us.

Aruno's voice blasted over the intercom. "Ambush! Take cover now!"

What lay in the wake around us were rigid airships, at least six our size. Then a swarm of twenty-seven smaller troop transports that flew near the large ships.

They didn't act like they noticed us, but they were too far away to examine closely. If they had noticed us, I'm sure their artillery ships could fire from a distance. I quickly snapped out of it, and hid behind a metal railing. I grabbed Satomi and yelled at her over the frantic noises around us. "Go to the bridge! We need to take cover now!"

Satomi started to run down the deck, but then stopped abruptly perhaps from shock. Sir Jonny was looking down from the bridge anxiety pinned his expression. He was waving at us to leave the area quickly and I could see the urgency in his eyes.

There was a flash of light, and the air was filled with smoke. Satomi flew backwards as I was thrown to the ground. The explosion was rapid, my ears ringing, making everything turn to white noise.

It took most of my effort to roll onto my stomach, place my hands below my torso and push myself up. I looked through the quickly dispersed smoke and found Satomi. Satomi, no... She wasn't moving. I ran over to her body and quickly shook her.

"Satomi!" My voice was barely audible over the ringing in my ears. She rolled over, revealing a large tear across her forehead; she must have been hit by flying debris. I quickly ripped up some ruffles from the side of her long skirt and wrapped it tightly around her forehead. I looked down at her; her chest was rising and falling slowly. She was still alive! I had hoped that she was only knocked out and not dying.

Every single horrible thing that had and could have happened to me, by far this had to have been the worst.

I looked around for a nearby medic. Through the chaos behind me I noticed a giant hole had been blasted through the bridge. I laid Satomi's back on the platform wall behind her. The stairs where now malformed and I placed each step with care. "Jonny!" I yelled out, searching for a reply. I made it to the above deck and ran to the cockpit being careful to avoid small fires that were littered about. Pirates laid all over the top deck, in different positions, not moving. It was a graveyard of souls.

I walked through burnt debris, the only thing that waited between the cockpit and the morning sky. The cockpit was now just a smoldering pile of timber in a remaining thin steel frame. I ran through the wrack. *Maybe he is still alive.*

When I looked through the side of the smaller cockpit area I saw Sir Jonny sitting with his back to the wall. His face awash with blood. The rest of him daubed with soot. Wounded skin and lesions damaged his body and his clothes were ripped in an unruly manner.

He grunted as he lamely threw a board that laid across his torso, onto the ground beside him. I ran to his side and grabbed his arm. He turned his head and met my gaze. He tried to wipe away the blood from his face in vain, only to leave it in more grime.

His face was twisted into a grimace as he spoke, "Where's" Sir Jonny cut off his words, and flinched with pain, as he nervously glanced around "Satomi."

I hadn't noticed that tears were running down my cheeks. "She's hurt pretty bad... but she's safe for now." I couldn't look him in the eye; I knew that he was slowly dying.

He spluttered, "Get her to safety." I was looking at his wounds when I noticed his right arm; it was completely gone, severed, and dripping with blood.

My eyes widened as I gaped in horror. "Jonny."

"Tell Aruno-" He coughed and blood spittled from his mouth. His voice trailed off, "Don't let them win." With that he collapsed back into a slump.

I couldn't let him die, I needed to run out of there and find medics for Sir Jonny and Satomi before they succumb to a worse fate. I would never forgive myself if that happened. I ran down the steps and crouched near Satomi. She was still, but breathing and the blood draining from her head had stopped.

I continued to the front deck. I saw Aruno messing with a metal grate that was attached to the floor. Within seconds a control module rose up to his height. I ran towards him and grabbed his shoulder. He turned to me with fear in his eyes, "What do you have to report?"

I said quickly. "Sir Jonny and Satomi need medics! Do you think we can fight our way out of this mess?"

His voice shook when he replied. "I'm not Captain Robert! We have to flee; the Annabeth wasn't built for sustained battle! Please, what about the others?"

I... I don't..." I couldn't get the words out.

He read my expression and registered what I meant to say. He quickly grabbed a communicator from his belt and yelled into it.

"Medical assistance to the bridge!"

He turned toward me and with a soft expression he explained. "This is going to get a lot worse and, I'm not so sure we're going to make it. If the worst does happen..." He paused and smiled. "Well, I wish I got to know you better." His smile faded abruptly. "The safest place for you right now is below deck, your mother would kill me if she found out you got hit by a stray bullet."

"okay," I said. *He must love my mother.* I quickly followed his orders and raced down the stairs. I stumbled sideways catching myself on the wall next to me, as a voice erupted from the intercom. "Forward, toward enemy fire!"

As I staggered into the lobby, a group of men in white were walking toward me. As they got closer I could hear them talking about the front of the ship being armored and that the ship could take a beating. One stopped as he noticed me, "Ma'am are you alright?" He spoke with sincerity in his voice. I quickly remembered how filthy I must have looked, compared to the whiteness of their suits. "I'm fine but... my friends. They need help. A young girl above deck named Satomi was hit pretty hard and Sir Jonny was in the bridge before it-"

His actions cut me off, he looked startled and ran toward upper deck, leaving me behind in the lobby. The Annabeth swung violently as it avoided the brunt of the fire. He was leading us closer to a battle we couldn't win! I looked out the window in the lobby. Some of them had been smashed. Most of the enemies' ships didn't have the range to reach ours, except for a few artillery. They fired at the Annabeth again but this time Aruno saw it coming and the volley deflected off the right side of the ship. At that time our focus was to escape the situation. We stayed at stratus level and were approaching a cloud on our left.

As we approached the front of the cloud, Aruno warned us of a left turn as we swung into it. This time however, the turn was less smooth and more jittery, because the new control panel being used wasn't elaborate enough to move the appropriate fins at the right time.

As we escaped through the clouds, I could see at minimum fifteen of the other ships heading in our direction fast. I looked into the mist blanketing us in a safety of invisibility against enemies at range. We were far from safe though, as this cloud cover could disappear at any time. At this time the crew was preparing for another attack by loading all the guns and taking people into the medical bay.

I saw Satomi then, being lifted in on a stretcher. I ran toward her, and asked the same medic I met earlier. "Is she okay?" They continued walking down the hall, leading to the medical room.

His voice sounded tired, "She looks to be okay, but we need to check her for brain damage."

"And Jonny?"

The man shook his head. "We're not sure." I was stopped in my tracks as they walked through another door. I was disappointed which made me angry. I wanted to know that they were okay, but of course what was I expecting. Sir Jonny had lost an arm, and he was near death last I saw him. And when Satomi was hit, I knew it was my fault. I was the one that told her to run. *Why did I say that?* It was in the past I needed to get over it. *Satomi will be fine, I know she will.* Everything was my fault.

The clouds started to thin out, and visible from the ships side the morning sky, bright orange, pink and white hues shown through the windows. The Annabeth pulled back into the open, after which, we found out we were in extensive agitation when two of the ships following us, pulled up on either side. A fire fight soon commenced and I ran to take cover, away from the windows. I waited in a stairwell, far from the windows yet, I made sure I could still see from them.

Someone shouted from the door leading to outside, "Cannons ready, both sides!"

Minutes later I could hear Aruno once again over the loudspeaker yelling, "Fire at will!"

I ran up the stairs to the first deck to see the volley. The cacophonous fire started. One of the ships returned cannon fire and the other one pulled up to avoid it. I quickly ran to the middle of the stairs to avoid the explosion. About halfway down the stairs I waited because I thought it was both good cover and had an easy escape. My logic paid off, because a cannon ball blasted through the windows and through the hallway at the bottom. It hit the opposing wall and after losing most of its momentum, bounced heavily to the ground.

I jumped back up the stairs in surprise. The volleys ended, and I went back up the deck to see the damage. Our ship was barely damaged compared to the ones beside it. The enemy's ship was properly decimated and was slowly drifting downwards.

Before we could get back into great new form for a new volley, another ship flew in beside us that I hadn't accounted for. They quickly fired a volley into our balloons before we could pull up beside them. The Annabeth had a multilayer balloon design which helped prevent two thirds of the gas from escaping from the punctured balloons.

We started sinking downward. Many pirates looked scared from the encounter but kept running around listening to orders being given.

A Raqoian pirate ran around shouting different orders at people. "Pump hot air into the remaining containers for some extra lift." The group he had talked to nodded and ran off to fulfill the command. "Troops, get rid of any excess weight. Any hover cycles left, need to be manned and flown to defend Annabeth." The group stood there for a moment as if they were processing the information, or they were afraid. "Now!" His voice thundered. The troops ran off to their stations.

Moments passed and soon a squadron of hover cycles and bikes flew up to the enemy ship and helped prevent another barrage. At the same time, our anti aircraft cannons were firing at full speed.

The bullets and volleys didn't smash their hull, but did penetrate the enemy ship's fins and flying vessels. A mid air dogfight took place between our hover vehicles and there older looking gyrocycles before ours could get to their ship.

The battle was short and violent, because they were out gunned, out maneuvered, and out manned. Two of our hover pilots were shot out of the sky. The enemies' gyrocycles were shot down by our expert pilots. We quickly tore through their meager air-to-air defense, with some help of our anti aircraft guns.

Mechanics were still working on fixing the holes in our balloons as we slowly drifted downward. I overheard someone saying the substitute gas would be the steam from our engines.

Our hoverbikes landed on the surface of their ship. The pirates shot some men off of deck. The ones who were shown mercy cowered, fleeing downstairs. Shortly after a few of their crew were thrown over the side. Their ship was being disabled, but the time was not there to take control. The men didn't try to salvage any supplies. I saw them running around deck, placing dynamite on their pylons, the rope that attached the balloon to their ship

When our pilots were on their hovercrafts and headed back a few meters away, they detonated the explosives. The airship separated into two sections, the balloon flew into the sky, the keel that plummeted downward, created a large splash as it hit the ocean.

We were not free from trouble yet, for the rest of the armada were close behind. We quickly maneuvered to avoid fire from the long range ships. This wasn't all too successful when a few more rounds found their mark. One of the pirates was thrown across the floor. He did not die however, moments later he fought to sit up.

A second escape was quickly thought of, as we maneuvered to face nearby clouds. As we approached, another three ships emerged from the layer, which forced us to turn quick. With the Annabeth's control center being less elaborate now, then before; our turn was wide and brought us into the range of their concentrated cannon fire.

"Brace for impact!" A pirate nearby called out. I ran back down the stairs, stopping at the middle like before out of fear.

The impact from the barrage slammed into the sides of the ship, decimating Annabeth's armor. Quite a few rides tore through our balloon canopy and we descended downward quicker than we had been. It made it difficult to recover from, if it came to that. We slowly accelerated downwards because of the leaks from the remaining balloons. I had a sickening feeling that the crew would be sucked off the deck by the rushing air, like the deaths from the other airships.

Holding my balance, I quickly ran to the top of the stairs to see how prepared they were. The pirates tied themselves to various rails with ropes around their waist. A burly pirate ran over to me, caring belts around one arm, and ropes around the other. He handed me a belt that was attached to a length of rope. I quickly put the belt around my waist the same time he tied the rope to the staircase railing. Then, he ran to the next pirate with the same restraint system.

The Annabeth started to pick up speed as we plummeted downward. Some men in front of me, wearing restraints, ran toward the side, and jumped off. In mid air they deployed parachutes and flew upward, off deck toward the balloon canopy above. They were commanded to patch the blasted balloons, and pump them with replacement helium. We accelerated slower, the horizon flattened and the ocean was drawing near.

My sickening stomach stayed put, thirty meters above the water; it still did not feel like we were going to survive the crash. I looked at Aruno, and saw him pull a lever. As he did, a number of huge parachutes fired from around the ship, slowing descend abruptly. I was pushed down onto a crouching position from the increase of gravity's force.

I stood up and leaned out the stairway. The world around us seemed to relax for a moment as we hung below the parachutes. Then we hit the sea, and salty water sprayed into the air, some getting onto the ship's deck. I backed into the staircase one last time, to avoid being tangled in layers of the parachute. I soon heard gears creaking as they turned. The massive parachutes covering the doorway; were pulled back to the side of the ship.

I knew airships were not entirely meant to work as actual 'boats of the sea' faring type, but we stayed afloat, and the Annabeth would have truly moved like one, if it wasn't for the holes along the side. I ran out on deck just as some nine pirates were running into the staircase leading to bottom deck. "Seal as many doors as you can!" One of them shouted. I looked away into the sky, only to see the armada of airships and troop transports descending toward us.

Aruno had the look of defeat, but I knew he wouldn't give up, men like him never give up.

His voice could be heard over the PA system once more, "We are not done fighting. My nephew has ruined everything I have held dear, and I will not let him win this easily. We will fight till we no longer have the ability to." He then quickly ordered the anti aircraft guns to start shooting at the smaller aircraft. I stayed hidden just at the top of the stairwell, which gave me a quick escape if I were in danger.

In the midst of the attack, a large rigid dirigible appeared from the clouds. It was larger than ours, and void-black. The design a red symbolic crow stretched outward, covering the balloons sides. The fuselage was a cube shape art deco design with golden tentacles decaled layering around the side of the ship. Poles extended from the sides.

I saw a glint from its front main section, and then artillery shells. Then it happened, so quickly. One by one, they took out our anti aircraft guns. Pirates dived from the sides, spilling onto the deck, as the guns exploded, blasting through the uproar. It was the most horrifying thing I had witnessed.

CHAPTER 15

Hope

*T*he rest of the ships stopped descending to our level as if an order was given. The behemoth quickly swept past the one we fired at, and approached our ship. For the first moment of the battle, Aruno looked like he wasn't sure of what to do, as if he was afraid.

He quickly pulled up the communicator device and calmly talked into it, "Second commanders come to the upper deck, all other shipmates go below and arm yourself with anything for close range fighting. Once you're ready, wait there until further instructions." He showed his wrath, "I have a feeling that Orfeo will want to taunt me personally, like the boastful little piece of vermin scum he is."

The pirates moved quickly as did the fast approaching black ship from above. The mother ship started to slow down, stopping about two-hundred meters above us. A small area along the side opened up, and about three troop carriers launched out. Their basic design was a small square boat with four rotors, one on each angle. On the top middle a small container of flotation gas held it a drift. There were also small gun openings where the soldiers had their weapons trained on us.

Pirates who were ordered to wait in the stairway, stood behind me and I felt like I was in the way. I walked out of the staircase and alongside the wall, toward the new control deck. I untied the rope from around my waist and threw it on the ground. I found a niche along the wall, behind a pillar and hid there. The second in command stood in a group around Aruno, near the control module.

Aruno held authoritative power in his voice, "Everyone stay calm and don't fire on them. They will believe we want to surrender. If we're lucky my dumb nephew will be want to confront us, and when he does, we can strike the fool once he lands."

I heard a loud whir from the troop transports as they positioned themselves above the middle of the ship and lowered onto the deck. All of Aruno's men stood still in the waiting, and the air around me felt tenser than when it was filled with war.

The doors on the carriers opened, and the soldiers filled out around the transports. The ending could go either way. If Orfeo wasn't on this transport, Aruno could fight them off, and win. But in the process the ship above would destroy the Annabeth and us in seconds. On the other hand, if Orfeo truly believes he has us surrounded in a forced surrender, and he stepped upon the Annabeth himself, then the ship wouldn't dare fire on us. Orfeo dying meant their livelihood jeopardized.

These few moments would decide our fate. The last soldier stepped out, and standing a few feet behind him, Orfeo. A younger man in Aruno's crew let out a sigh at the sight of the king; but was quickly silenced as the man next to him slapped his hand over the kid's mouth, and shot him a disgusted look.

Orfeo dressed decadently, with a black and red tailcoat and ruffled ascot underneath. He held a black metallic helmet under his arm. His stature was incredibly intimidating. He looked proud to have found his uncle, what an accomplishment for him. The knights stepped aside as their king calmly walked to the front of the ranks.

"You knew that I was going to find you at some point, this was really your inevitability. However you are not the one I am after. Where is my brother?"

Aruno was the only one who dare speak, "He is long gone, probably finding that damned will that you hid like a coward."

"Your taunts do not threaten me. As of my brother? I would have been told of his defying stunts."

Aruno retorted, "Signals cannot reach this far out." He laughed, "He might even be taking over your empire as we speak."

Orfeo face contorted into vexation. He responded with an order to his Nobles' "We're leaving. Capture Aruno and anyone who resists."

Aruno grinned as he lifted the intercom to his lips, "It's time. Attack!"

Pirates swarmed from all the stairwells around the ship, and rushed toward the guards and soldiers, surrounding them. The pirates on deck stood in fighting stance, waiting for their orders.

Orfeo yelled. "Give up! You can't win this. We already have more soldiers than you." He half chuckled. "And if that's not enough, more will be flown in."

"Ground the transport ships, don't let him escape."

With that the pirates in the front ducked down. The pirates in the back fired their weapons into the soldiers' ranks. The soldiers were then disoriented and a number of them were injured with gunfire. The crouching pirates dived into their ranks, swords drawn. This coordinated attack around the tightly bunched soldiers were enough to properly disrupt their ranks.

Orfeo was on his way back to the center transport ship when a pirate signaled to the group near the stairway and suddenly, five pirates pulled a cannon from below deck. Then one of the first mates called for the pirates on the front line of battle to form a divide, as the cannon wouldn't hit any of Aruno's pirates.

They rapidly separated in a line from the cannon to the middle transport. The soldiers were confused by this for they were prioritized by the pirates attacking them. The cannons were fired and the volley slammed through their ranks, destroying their transport.

Orfeo was about ten feet away from the explosion. He staggered back and put his arm over his face to protect himself from the heat. He quickly tried to regain his composure till he noticed that his hair was on fire, which he quickly put out, probably hopping no one had noticed.

He quickly pulled his sword out to look more commanding. I could see him mouth, "Take the canons." Our pirates were making their way into the ranks of soldiers, but we were still outnumbered three-to-one. The air was filled with smoke from gunfire and the floors glistened with blood which streaked along the grooves.

The pirates who fought the Raqoian Noble guards seemed to be equally matched. Five soldiers from the back line, unexpectedly charged through the front line of pirates.

More pirate reinforcements closed the hole in the front of the line. Out of these five soldiers, three were quickly shot down where they stood. The other two—, who were smart, dived behind cover. Aruno ran and jumped over a barricade toward one of the soldiers, and quickly slashed the man down.

The other soldier pulled a pistol and aimed it at Aruno, even though he probably couldn't hit Aruno from his range. Aruno quickly rolled behind the barricade as the soldier pulled the trigger, firing in his general area. Then the soldier quickly ran for a trap door. Bullets from riflemen in higher sections pinged around him as he opened it, and descended below. There was a small group of pirates sent down to root him out.

More pirates ran beside me, down another set of stairs. I backed up and placed my back on the wall behind me. The wall moved backward as I did causing my body to jerk startled. The wall made a low rumbling sound and moved sideways. I turned around frantic.

The moved wall opened a new staircase. The war in front of me was only getting worse and bullets flew by my head. I turned around and walked slowly down the dark staircase. I stopped close to the top, just enough to hide from open fire. I stayed there for a couple of minutes until louder fire erupted. As I backed down a stair I was grabbed violently from behind.

I let out a small scream before the man slapped a hand over my mouth, placing a gun to my head. I had hoped someone heard my screech but I doubt it mattered.

"Shut-up, they won't kill me if I have some girl hostage!" He spat into my ear. The man holding me put his back against the wall. I tried struggling but I couldn't and I gave up. I looked down the stairs and a pirate ran down the perpendicular hallway.

He glimpsed the soldier and threw himself with his back to hallway entrance. He returned a moment later with back up as they pulled around both corners, guns drawn pointed at the soldier.

The pirate who had noticed me demanded, "Let go of the girl, and you can walk freely!" His accent was Vermyrian, and looked the part.

"You lying scumbags, I'll kill her if you don't lower your weapons!" The man countered. We then found ourselves in a stalemate. I bit his hand, but the only reaction he gave was to grab me around the neck.

I felt the pain of being a weakness to the pirates again. *I'm sick of being a burden.* I needed to solve this myself. I soon thought of a plan.

I pulled my teddy up to my belt, so it would cover the pocket with the gun Satomi gave me. I quickly pretended to put my other hand around the teddy bear. I then slipped my hand under it, grabbing the gun handle and put my finger on the trigger.

I felt the gun for a safety button of some sort so I could fire. I then pulled back the hammer slowly like I had seen so many other pirates do. I muffled the click with my teddy bear. The soldier continued arguing with the pirates, "Go ahead, and try it!" He yelled in frustration. His grip loosened, probably from believing I wouldn't do anything to stop him.

I struggled and looked up at him, "Please let me go!"

"Shut up!"

I then pushed my gun from under my bear and pointed the end at his feet. I slightly turned my head away as I fired the trigger. There was a flash and a deafening noise. The soldier screamed in agonizing pain, as he released me and fell sideways, his gun falling down the stairs. I had grazed his shin and blasted his foot. Blood seeped on the stairs underneath me. I turned around, and held my gun pointed at him, my hands shaking. Some pirates from the bottom ran up and pointed their own guns at him.

I backed down the stairs and let them handle it. As the soldier's voice faded I could hear cheering from a man behind me.

Tears streaked my cheeks. *I acted like a killer, I'm just like them.* He was going to sacrifice me to survive a few more moments. Of course he was going to kill me, there was no doubt of it, but as long as I was alive, his life would have been spared. I knew that the reason I had done it was because after I asked him sincerely he ignored my plead.

The man, who had cheered minutes before, walked up to me and gave me a hug, lifting me from the ground. "Good job, you did it!"

"Um..." He put me back down, "Thank you..."

"I saw when you put the gun behind the bear, very smart of you. If one of us shot him first, we could have struck you by accident."

I felt uncomfortable and at this point I needed to be separated from people. "Right, well, we need to get back to the fight at hand." I wasn't trying to be rude; I was just uncomfortable with people after what I had done.

"Righty-o" He patted me on the head and walked up the stairs with the rest of the backup crew. After we separated, I decided I should get to the aft of the ship. The aft was higher than the war occupied ship. From the height I could get a good view of the battle going on below. As I made my way through different hallways, I almost found myself getting lost. Midsection shelves of books in the library were underwater but protected by metal walls.

It made me feel a bit better that I had left the book here, knowing that it wouldn't be ruined. I continued down the hall, and found a ladder that lead to the aft and made my way up. I opened the door and saw Orfeo's armada had drawn in close. *We're going to get over ran by them if they land on the Annabeth! What are we going to do!* The entire war now seemed nearly useless.

I pulled myself out of the trap door and lowered the hatch. Next to me, on deck I saw about six pirates with long rifles aiming down and firing at the soldiers and Nobel guards. *All of this war and bloodshed, and for what? To find Kazuhiko who was long gone by now.* I ran to the edge of the deck to see the battle unfold below me.

One of the snipers fired and a soldier left of the transports dropped dead. I saw another one trained on Orfeo, but he kept himself protected by bulletproof armor and surrounded by Nobel guards.

I looked up to see another troop transport descending about one-hundred meters away. I saw the pirates on the front of the ship pulling a cannon from the lower deck and aiming it. The cannon was quickly lit and fired, hitting one of the rotor axes, debilitating it and sending it veering into the sea. The ship didn't sink, but they were stranded until further help from the armada, which wouldn't be long.

We were forty seconds away from being overwhelmed with low flying hover vehicles and troop transports being dispatched from the many ships above. Soon after that, the rest of the slower attack ships would arrive.

As another troop transport approached close behind, above the last ship that was struck down; I saw a glint out of the corner of my eye. The transport ship was destroyed and fell from the sky, but it wasn't the pirates who destroyed it. I looked in the direction of where the shot came from to see a second armada of ships approaching. Raqoian imperial flags flew, but never the less they started to engage on Orfeo's armada.

I looked below to see general confusion for anyone who wasn't directly fighting and cheering from the pirate ranks. Orfeo was yelling furiously into a handset, I couldn't hear him from this distance, but I knew what he was talking about.

The battle above was furious, and the debris peppered the ocean. The battle on our ship was over though. The pirates seemed to be making headway and the baffled soldiers were losing men. Orfeo knew that his overconfidence with his men that they could win even surrounded was falsely placed.

He ordered the remaining soldiers to all move outboard to starboard so they could get out of their surrounded situation. The left of the regiment broke through the lines of pirates which freed the soldiers to spread along the port side. The pirates formed into a line and rushed back into battle with the soldiers. The soldiers rushed into battle as well leading to, instead of a group on group battle, a freer fighting melee.

Aruno ordered the pirates that were keeping their distance to shoot the soldiers and join the fray, fearing that his crew might shoot a friend in the confusion.

A few kept their post but the rest rushed in. Aruno followed them into the cacophony of violence, and showed his prowess with a sword, swiftly downing two soldiers with multiple strikes. It was apparent that he was then making his way to Orfeo.

I looked up to see that the battle between the empire ships had stopped. The newly arrived ships had dominated a few of the middle ships, but I still didn't understand why they attacked in the first place, and why the attack stopped.

It confused me but I was more interested in the fight between Aruno and Orfeo so I trained my attention back on them. I looked down to see Orfeo throw his handset into the deck, smashing it to pieces from anger.

He then turned to the direction of Aruno who had carved a swath through the soldiers standing in his way. Orfeo was surprised by this and hurriedly pulled out a long sword and assuming a defensive position. Aruno stepped in close with his thin sword taking a fencer's stance. They circled for a few moments. Orfeo swung from the right, but Aruno deflected it up and countering swiftly, stabbed at Orfeo. The king dodged sideways and the attack grazed off his armor.

This sent Aruno forward with the momentum of the strike. Orfeo, now facing his side, swung for his exposed back. Aruno used the momentum from his missed strike to jump up and launch himself off the portside railing, back over the direction of Orfeo's swing. He expertly spun in the air, aiming an uppercut strike at the lower part of the King's helm. Orfeo, not expecting this elaborate move, didn't react fast enough to avoid the hit.

The sword flung the helmet off Orfeo's head and sent it flying, but more importantly revealed a weakness, Orfeo's face and neck. The helmet landed on the ground, at the same time as Aruno, who rushed at the helmet and kicked it off the ship to keep Orfeo vulnerable to attack.

Aruno turned back around to face the enraged King. Orfeo pulled a pistol from a leg side compartment, while Aruno swiftly jumped for cover behind two barrels to avoid the gunfire. Once crouched behind the barrels, he prepared a gun of his own, turned, and aimed his gun at Orfeo's head.

The two stood in deadlock for a few seconds, thinking intensely of what their next move for attack would be. Deciding almost in unison the two pulled their triggers. Smoke filled the air around them both as the pistols sounded. They looked confused for a second, not knowing if they had suffered fatal injury.

Orfeo checked his ear to find a chunk of it had disappeared, but Aruno wasn't injured.

They quickly engaged in sword battle once again. Orfeo was more defensive knowing he had a weakness. He focused on defensive strikes and not over extending himself with wide movements. Aruno was furiously trying to break Orfeo's defense and strike his neck. The king ducked back to maintain some breathing room. Aruno eagerly tried to close this gap, but Orfeo fended him off with his long sword.

They circled at sword length.

"Orfeo, you're never going to win this. To me, it looks like my men are winning, while you haven't laid a hand on me."

Orfeo answered in a condescending tone, "You honestly think you could beat me without some sort of fictitious luck? As soon as my fleet arrives, I'll have outgunned you about a thousand times over."

"You seem to be fighting pretty defensively, nephew." Aruno laughed.

With that, Orfeo stabbed forward. Aruno expected this attack, and dodged left, in the hopes that Orfeo would compromise his defective position by following the momentum of the sword strike, following Aruno's past moves.

Orfeo noticed this as well, because he pulled his stab early. Then to trap Aruno, Orfeo grabbed the side of his own sword and transferred his grip from the handle to the flat side of the blade, transferring his stance perpendicular to the sword. He used the long sword like a pole to pin Aruno against the ship's railing knocking his sword out of his hands. Aruno maneuvered and kicked Orfeo off of him, but did not push him far enough that Orfeo couldn't be in range to strike immediately again.

Orfeo used his momentary advantage to swing at Aruno while he was down. I wasn't sure Aruno could dodge out of the way this time, if he did in either direction, he would still be in the arc of Orfeo's swing.

Melvin ran and jumped towards Orfeo, tackling him mid swing and enveloping him in layers of body fat. Orfeo fell and was trapped by the cooks quite immense body.

Aruno picked up his sword and ran over to the struggle; he slipped his sword next to Orfeo's neck. "Melvin…" He wasn't responding. "Zayne! Conner! Help Melvin!" The two pirates, who weren't participating in the battle, ran over to pull Melvin off Orfeo.

They rolled him over to find Orfeo's long sword firmly lodged in his sternum. Melvin gasped as blood leaked from the wound. Aruno was appalled in shock.

Orfeo, noticed Aruno was distracted and tried to get away. Aruno turned back to him, "I wouldn't do that if I were you." He gestured at the two pirates. "Tie him up; we'll let the empire deal with him once they know the truth."

Beside Aruno, Melvin coughed and seemed like he was regaining consciousness. Aruno hurried over to his side.

Melvin breathily exclaimed, "I saved ya, capt'n."

Aruno smiled nervously, "That you did… The entire crew will be thankful."

"We might lose in the long run... now that we haven't a cook." Melvin morbidly joked.

Aruno didn't care too much about joking. "I'll send medics, but I'm afraid there's nothing they can do in this situation..."

Melvin wheezed. "Just try to stay alive, and hire a good cook, I'm glad I could be of service to you." Aruno smiled at him one last time before he rushed off to protect his crew from Orfeo as they walked him to the back of the Annabeth.

He held a sword to the King's neck. Orfeo spat, "They're not going to believe you. You're a traitor."

"No? But they will believe Kenzai and your brother." Orfeo gaped and looked away furious. The battle raged beside them as they walked him towards crew waiting.

The distracted soldier's group thinned in numbers as some fell to the ground injured, knocked out but rarely killed.

Crew stood around Orfeo to defend him from the soldiers wishing to rescue their leader, none were successful. They stopped near a transport surrounded by a plateau of boxes and yelled, "We have your king! Drop your weapons or we keep his head as a trophy!"

Their threat worked and one-by-one the soldiers dropped their weapons. The rambunctious exuberant pirates cheered from all around and most standing soldiers clapped their hands or looked grateful to be alive. Most from both sides celebrated their victory.

Aruno stood at the makeshift helm that was created and waved his arms as to silence the celebration. The crew understood what he was doing.

He pulled a communicator toward him and yelled into it what I assumed to be a military signal. "Stand down! We have your king, and we won, do not pursue with further attack!" He released the button and everyone waited in anticipation of the resulting answer.

"I told you I was capable."

"Kazuhiko?" Aruno was shocked but figured as much.

"I'm guessing you were wondering why there was a battle between the empire and itself."

Aruno was annoyed, "I'll have to admit it to you, I'm glad you disobeyed my orders."

"I have found the will and the empire has agreed to comply too my orders!"

The entire ship flooded with cheers once more, everyone this time cheered, all the pirates and soldiers. All, but Orfeo, who was taken in the transport system, the doors closed.

"Is Zathena alive?" A pirate nodded toward Aruno.

"Yes. She should be somewhere..." Aruno looked around and spotted me, standing on the overlay near the additional gun shooters. I smiled at him and he explained into the device, "Get down here, you have to see her, she's turned into a real pirate recently!"

CHAPTER 16

It Ends

*K*azuhiko walked onto deck from the broadside entrance and onto the wrecked Annabeth. His smile brightened when he saw me standing amid ship. He bolted toward me held me close embracing me. I couldn't stop laughing as he lifted me off of the deck and kissed my cheek.

"Zathena!" he sat me back down.

"I didn't know what to do when you left me back there!"

He looked confused for a second, "In the city?"

I smiled, "yea."

"Where I was going, you'd have been safer here." Kazuhiko grabbed the shoulder of the nearest soldier. "Get back to the ship, tell the Nobles to call, and have Kenzai released from jail. Tell them to bring her to the castle in Versalen, I'll meet her there." The guard nodded his head and ran towards the edge of the deck. He got on a gyrocycle and flew off to Kazuhiko's empire airship.

Kazuhiko hugged me again, holding me close. "I'm so glad you're alive."

"Without you, we wouldn't have survived."

"I'm surprised you have little faith in Aruno's ability." I smiled then he pulled away. "I need to fly back to Versalen. Please promise me you'll meet me there."

"I promise," I smiled again. "I can't wait to meet your sister. I hope she's okay."

He smirked. "I need to leave; don't get in trouble." Kazuhiko let go of me and stepped into the opening of the royal transport, elaborate metalwork decorated the sides of a longer sleeker, pointed vessel designed differently from any other standard transport ship.

I left the boat from the side, walking down a bridge that connected onto the shore. Aruno stood facing the Annabeth, his expression was downcast. I've never seen him this sad before. I walked up to him and stood next to him in silence. I didn't exactly know what to say to him, it was as if taking in the silence around us was the only thing that could cure our insanity. He continued his gaze and spoke with no emotion. "I couldn't save them."

"Aruno..."

"One hundred of my men died, and I couldn't save them. In return, we killed a mass number of Raqoians...my own. This entire war was for nothing. "

I joked around thinking that it would make him feel better. "They were only a few imperialist dogs."

"No," He shook his head, still looking at the wreck of the Annabeth. "They were humans. They deserved the right to live just as I do; and I took that away from them." He finally broke his locked gaze from the ship, pulled out a gun from his holster and studied it closely. Turning it loosely in his hands, looking at the sides of it. He sighed and threw it into the ocean.

He turned to hug me, his strong embrace startled me. I hugged him back and said, "I thought you weren't going to make it."

He glimpsed down at me, "For a moment there, I thought I wasn't either."

"I'm happy I can call you my step-father."

He smiled at me, "The crew and I will find your mother, and you won't have to be afraid or worry anymore."

I backed away, "I can help too you know?"

"My crew can handle this. Also, I heard you stole a gun from the armory?"

I pulled the gun from my bag. "No I didn't, Satomi gave this to me."

"And did you shoot someone's foot with it?" He asked with his eyebrow raised.

"Sort of. If it happens again, I might just let them shoot me instead."

He took the gun from my hand and threw it into the watery depths below. As it sunk he explained, "It was an old model anyway." I was baffled. I knew he had other guns on him, but I guess throwing his weapons into the ocean made him feel less villainous. "They told me that Sir Jonny might not make it. He hasn't regained consciousness yet, and I'm not sure that he will."

I was shocked. I placed my hand through my hair; trying to hold back tears. I knew it was going to happen. Everything I had went through this day, and now Jonny was going to die. It was hard for me to think about it, his smile and the way he spoke. He was my friend and now... I may never speak to him again.

Aruno continued, "Satomi might wake up soon. We should be there when she does." We turned around and headed off toward a towering red and white lighthouse. "After the Annabeth fell into the ocean, we had the wounded flown to the nearest clean building. Homes around here normally have sand floors. We couldn't risk that." I didn't feel like talking; I walked in silence.

Once we reached the lighthouse Aruno looked slightly concerned. "After Satomi wakes up, I need to tell her... I just need you, to let me speak to her first."

I nodded. The door was opened from the inside and we walked in. Satomi tried to sit up, but gave up in the process and laid back down. "Hi guys." she smiled in a daze. It sounded as though she was completely out of it. Aruno sat in a chair beside her bed. "How're you feeling kid?" He smiled, trying to ignore the blood stains on her forehead. Her smile twitched a bit as she talked. "I'm okay, just tired."

"I spoke to the doctors about Sir Jonny. They said... he might not make it."

"I've seen him. He'll come out of it, he always does."

"Satomi, there is something he wanted me to tell you. He didn't quite know how to explain it to you." He spoke somberly, "He wanted to tell you that he was a failure at being a parent, and that he loved you, but he couldn't face himself to tell you the truth. It was hard for him."

"Sir Jonny is..." She thought for a moment. "My dad?" Her eyes widened in surprise and her smile grew. "That's so cool." Her excitement drained every inch of her energy and she fell back asleep. Aruno got up and walked back toward me. I would have never been able to guess what he told her. It was astounding.

He placed his hand on my shoulder and spoke quietly. "She won't be too happy about that tomorrow I suppose." Right before we left a medic walked toward us, blocking our way out. "We've found the Steel Elements sir. They are confirmed dead. We found their carcasses in the basement."

"I hope so." I spoke breathlessly.

"They are a loss, and I feel bad for losing them, however, they weren't the same people I first hired. They took their experiments a bit too far for my liking."

"I would have to agree with you Captain."

"Aruno," I tugged on his sleeve. "Kazuhiko told us to meet him at the castle in Versalen."

"Keep an eye on Jonny. We will be back later for Satomi and Jonny hopefully." The medic nodded his head and left to attend to Satomi.

It took a while before we were ready to go. Aruno called for a transport system for us and a few other pirates. Once the transport system arrived and the doors opened, Argo shouted from the side, "Aruno! Been a long time hasn't it?" He let out a joyous laugh.

"It sure has Argo!" As Aruno walked up into the transport they gave each other a friendly hug.

Argo continued, "When you shot down the Empire's airship, it was magnificent." Argo looked over at me, "I'm guessing you did find her then?"

Aruno joked, "She's more trouble than it's worth."

"I can still hear you…" I glowered.

Argo laughed, "It was merely a joke lass, come on lets head off to the castle!"

I jumped on board with them and sat down in a seat near the side. Kadon, Aunna and Garron sat near me. Kadon asked, "What was it like fighting on an airship?"

"Did you ever get in the way?" Aunna interjected.

"HEY YOU GUYS SHUT UP! Did you kill anyone?"

After I answered their questions and not-so-questions we didn't really talk for the rest of the trip.

*   *   *   *   *

We arrived at the castle; the walls loomed above us, shadowing streets behind us. The garden in front, lined the edges of the wall, looked vibrant after the heavy rainfall. Raqoian flags hung on all walls of the castle's hallways. Aruno stopped by a large door halfway down the hall and gestured us through. Kazuhiko and Kenzai stood near each other by the massive windows, looking our way. Kenzai's smile brightened. "Aruno," Her long auburn hair swiftly moved behind her as she walked up to him slowly and caressed his face with her hand, you would have never been able to tell she was held in a prison for four years. Her dress was beautiful, an aquamarine high-low dress, clingy around the waist with silver lace down the back. "I'm glad you are alright, I've missed you so much."

Aruno almost had tears in his eyes, he hugged her "It's been forever, I know. I'm so sorry."

Kenzai nearly jumped when she saw me. "You are Zathena? Kazuhiko has told me so much about you." She smiled as her eyes turned a bit grey, she clasped my hand between hers, "You are naive, emotional, and downhearted," I felt offended until she continued, "but you are also brave, intelligent, and stronger than you know." She nodded, "Thank you for helping Kazuhiko and for trying to save me."

"You are welcome, it was really nothing."

Aruno barged in, "Again, she is more trouble than needed."

I glowered for a short minute. "If Orfeo is locked in jail, does this mean you're now the Queen over Vermyria?"

"No... unfortunately when he forced me to sign over the legal documents, he will remain king until he signs them back over to us."

"However," Kazuhiko interrupted, "the council has spoken, he will no longer be in charge of Vermyria, nor will he live in Raqoia. The guards must follow Kenzai and I rather than just Kenzai. The Raqoian council has ordered him to sign over the documents and if he doesn't comply... who knows what will happen."

Argo asked. "What about Orfeo's wife? Can't she do anything?"

I was flabbergasted. "Orfeo has a wife?"

Aruno laughed, "I mean, I thought I knew nothing about politics." I ignored his jokes.

"Yes my brother's wife," Kazuhiko thought for a moment then said, "I heard they've been fighting more recently. Unnie will most likely never help him out of this."

"I guess he is really gone..." Argo explained.

Aruno interjected once more, "You're guessing this? He killed my brother. Moments ago he tried his hand at killing me as well, his uncle."

Kazuhiko waved at the nearest Noble who then walked over to us, "We need to give a speech tomorrow to all the citizens of Vermyria. The gates are not allowed closed, food needs to be provided and every guard needs to hand out personal invitations to everyone's household."

"We will get right on the preparations sire!" The Noble walked out of the room. When Kazuhiko ordered the guard my first immediate thought was; *I think I'm getting over my fear of Raqoia.* I felt relieved.

"I have a wonderful proposal!" Kenzai burst. "Let's have a large commemoration for the pirates and guards who have survived the strife."

"I don't know if that's a good idea. My crew, are pirates for a reason."

Kenzai laughed, "Your crew were former Raqoians I'm sure they can impersonate well behaved people for one night."

"You have a point, my crew does love to party, and I'm sure they'd love to join, as long as they can provide the music."

"This is marvelous!" Losing her cool composure Kenzai practically leaped into Aruno's arms, "The guests are to wear their best formal attire, it will be ravishing!"

"It's settled then," Argo explained while swigging a glass of wine, "Celebration time!" He threw the glass to the ground and it shattered into a million pieces.

"Zathena, let me dress you?" Kenzai hooked my arm and we left down the hallway and entered into one royal red room. It had one large flag hanging above a black canopy bed. Kenzai walked to a door at the far end of the room, leaving me to close the door behind us.

She opened up the wooden door and gestured me to follow her. I was sort of confused but I followed, nonetheless. The door she opened was a full length walk-in closet. Long dresses covered every wall. One dress in particular caught my eye, long silk ruffled blue dress, which pinned up revealing black ruffles underneath. The top was a corset with a nice bow on the side. Kenzai chose the same dress but in a dark green color.

*   *   *   *   *

The dance that night was set up like nothing I had ever seen. The golden painted walls were adorned with jewels of every type and color. The golden chandeliers were hanging and placed about on the ceiling, every few feet. Everyone looked royal, but the pirates. They looked as 'royal' as they could be, suits and bow ties, nothing extremely fancy. The pirates were playing sea shanties on stage, and the crowd was riled in dance.

The bartender, Donna, was still alive! And pouring drinks for men by the dozen. Her 'pirate friend', stood by her side, skinny, ripped pants and a black leather jacket, long crimped dirty blonde hair and the look of excitement. He was not even dressed for a party but looked nice standing there next to her.

While my thoughts were occupied, Kazuhiko walked up next to me, "You're more radiant tonight then I have ever seen." He wore a bespoke long sleeved gray chalk stripe double-breasted suit. With a peaked lapel and waistcoat.

His words caught me off guard. No one had ever complimented me like that before. I wasn't even thinking when I joked, "It's a wonder what a bath can do, huh?"

"You're adorable." He laughed. A group of couples danced past us, their wife's long hair in a half pinned back up do, long elegant dresses none as extravagant as mine.

"I don't feel right being here without Satomi, she would have loved this."

"We shall throw Satomi her own party. One more extravagant than this. Do you think she will enjoy that?"

"She would love that..." I found myself smiling again.

"Would you," His voice was calm, like he had asked so many girls before me; "like to dance?"

I tensed, "No... I've never danced before, I don't even know how to."

He smiled, "I'll teach you." He led me by the hand and we walked to the center floor. He removed his top hat and bowed, which lead me confused and I just froze there. *This is a horrible idea.*

Kazuhiko put his hand on the middle of my back and pulled me near him. He loosely held my hand outward. His posture was strong while mine was sloppy. My arm rested on his and he raised my elbow up with his, and left mine higher. *I can do this, I can do this.* We waltzed in a circle. *I'm actually dancing with the prince? Left back, right right, right front, left left, left back, right right, left- oh no I stepped on his toe.* "Uhh... sorry."

Not making a scene he laughed quietly. "It's fine, honestly."

I giggled nervously. "Alright…" While we continued to dance the room and lights were spinning around us. How we could have danced so elegantly to sea shanties was beyond me, but it was such a perfect moment.

After a couple of minutes of pure delightment, the music died down. Kazuhiko and I stopped dancing and noticed the band was taking a short break. The leader of the band was Vermyrian and wore a kilt with his suit jacket. He lifted a megaphone to his mustache covered mouth, "We all know who the royal couple is tonight!" The crowd around us clapped their hands in abundance of joy. The Raqoians must have really wanted Kazuhiko as their king. *Everyone thinks we are dating? I mean, I know he likes me but why would they declare this at a celebration for them?* Even Aruno looked happy. I blushed from embarrassment and never noticed how shaken I was.

Kazuhiko whispered near my ear, "Do you want to get out of here?" I nodded and followed him out the way we came.

We walked down a few different hallways, guards stood at every corner. "The Raqoians usually involve themselves in royal arrangements. I hope you don't mind," I didn't answer him, and I stopped by the end of the hall. He looked down at me, and asked sincerely, "Are you okay?"

"Of course? I mean… yea. They were all looking at me… and"

Kazuhiko's cheeks flushed and he swiftly grabbed me around my waist, as he brought his face closer to mine;

grinning. The machine work in his eye became visible, copper wires enticed around a faint red glow that flickered around his metal pupil. Realizing I was staring straight into his beautiful mechanical and blue eyes, I looked away from him, I could have pushed him away, but It wasn't that easy.

I felt my cheeks flush a pink color as he pulled me closer, "I think I've fallen for you. I can't live without you." His face was so close to mine that I could feel the air off of his words. Just when the longing started to become unbearable, Kazuhiko placed his lips on mine. The warmth of his mouth sent an electric current down my spine, his lips were soft and I somehow found myself enjoying this moment. I pulled away, my heart fluttering.

Boots stomped down the hallway, Kazuhiko and I looked to the right, away from the party, then let go of me, when armored personnel walked towards us.

"Zilpher?" I shouted. "You're alive?!" He stood in front of a blinding light, and at first I didn't know what it could have been.

Kazuhiko's mechanical eye flashed red and he held the look of fear in his eyes. He whispered, "I thought the Steel Elements were dead?!" I noticed them then. They walked closer to us, my own fearful reflection brought back to me by the mirrored mask.

Kazuhiko grabbed me by the arm and pulled me with him as we ran separately, down the adjoining hallway.

"Grab them." and with Zilpher's order the sadistic knight bolted down the hallway. Soon followed by the man with the electrical gauntlet, who, sprinted faster than we could, but not as fast as the knight.

After he caught up, he extended his metal arm in front of him and stretched his bent fingers out. Electricity arced from his gauntlet and latched onto Kazuhiko. He tensed and jerked as the electricity went through him, locking every muscle in his body. Guards stood by the wall, not moving.

As he fell back, I tried to run after him, only to be grabbed by the knight himself.

"Kazuhiko!" I screamed. The man that held me gave me no freedom of movement.

As he regained his footing on his own, the mirror masked medic stood over him, with vials in his hand, and looking down at him, tilting his head from side to side, as he thought of something. Kazuhiko backed up to the cornered wall, frightened.

The Steel Elements were his true fear.

The man with the gauntlet walked forward and the rest of the over powered Elements surrounded us. "Why are you doing this!?" I cried.

"There are powers at play that you couldn't begin to understand."

A low rumbling sound erupted from beyond the wall behind the Steel Elements. The metal armored soldiers fell over. The men I thought were the guards of the castle were only empty standing suits on display.

Zilpher looked frightened and explained, "its here, this can't be happening."

It happened in a sudden instant. A glowing orb flashed in front of me, the walls changed around me, the castle deteriorated into crumbling brick but then rebuilt around us.

My temples thumped in pain and it felt like I was knocked in the head. What I thought were the walls turned colors, like something I had never seen before. It fell around me once more, and fire raged through the city beyond me, intense heat filled the room then it rebuilt again.

The ceiling turned to metal and seeped water. The window behind us became a doorway to the ocean, and burst; water flooded down the hallway but then disappeared without touching us. Then everything went dark.

I awoke, my headache burned and throbbed. I could barely see the hands in front of me. The Steel Elements laid on the ground, unmoving. Kazuhiko sat up beside me, unhurt. Zilpher stood up, unfazed and stared at the thing in front of us all.

A column of reflective glass appeared; a recess in the mirrored surface outlined a door which began to open.

Acknowledgements

There are so many people I want to thank for helping me finish my life's work. When I first began writing this series I was just a small girl of age 13 sitting in a boring classroom. I use to play games out on the playground with my dear friend Myckenzie Gatten. She helped me write the first draft of this book which later went on to being the first outline. She has helped me since.

My school Columbus Signature Academy is a new tech school and they really paved the way into helping me follow my dreams during my senior project! Without their approval I would have never been given the confidence or reliance to finish this book. I never thought attending this certain high school could open up so many doors for me.

Another individual I would like to thank would be Joshua Bederaux-cayne. Does the name sound somewhat familiar? Yea, there is a street named after him in the first chapter.

And rightfully so.

He and I have been through so much stress writing this book and now he understands what skills it takes in writing a novel and also how much support one needs. He helped write, or rather, he wrote chapters 12, 14, and 15. Without his help in editing and further instructional help I'm not sure I would have ever finished the book.

Sebastian Miller edited and sat in at every group meeting and he even helped create the Abutyus tree! There is nothing this lad can't do and I know he will follow his dreams one day, just as he has helped me follow mine!

Justin Monroe has help with formatting and has written a few important parts like the synopsis! I'm glad I added him into the group!

Finally and somewhat regrettably I would like to mention "Jonathan Sanders" for his help in mentoring me. I wish that we didn't leave on such bad terms.

I normally always give up but I've had friends, teachers and family that have pushed me to my limits with finishing what I started. Tammy Litten; is Joshua's mentor and she has helped us significantly. She has edited, read, and reviewed the entire book before it was ever finished. When she reads the final product I know she will be impressed.

Rachelle Antcliff is our English 12 teacher; she helped us in any way that she could. All from disagreeing group members to impossible to work with members. I'm glad I can mention her.

And Mike Reed; our principle, who had helped us with giving us an 'okay' to working on this product and I couldn't be happier.

On to the bigger mentions! I'm so proud of myself to be mentioning this next person. He has inspired me time and again, I cannot be more ecstatic! Toby Lawhon is a wonderful musician, poet and writer. The band Marquis of Vaudeville inspired me before the writing of this novel, and his okay to letting me use his persona as a fictitious character in my book truly helped me in creating a non-forgettable character

Last but never least; thank you for the ones who have bought this book. I know many of you have inspired me to create characters and I thank you for that. Please never stop dreaming! You can accomplish anything in the entire world if only you'd just believe in yourself!

Zathena and the Sky Pirates
THE END

...or is it,
The Institution of M.A.S.A.
coming Fall of 2016